Surviving

the

Darkest

Days

Tonetta Chester

Surviving the Darkest Days

Published by TC Publishing Group®
2870 Peachtree Road, Suite 616
Atlanta, GA 30305-2918 U.S.A.
www.tcpublishinggroup.com

International Standard Book Number: 978-1-93571-407-1
Library of Congress Control Number: 2007940639

This book is a work of fiction. All names, characters, places, and incidents are purely fictional. Any resemblance to any actual events, locales, or persons, living or dead, actual events, establishments, organizations, and locales are intended to give the fiction a sense of reality and authenticity and are coincidental. Other names, characters, places, events, and incidents are either products of the author's imagination or are used fictitiously.

Cover by: Distinctive Creations

In loving memory of
Jerriff Omar Harper
October 29, 1981–October 30, 2006

I love you!

Thank you for the memories that we shared. I love you and wish you were here. I miss you so much, Chuck!

Don't forget to tell the people that you love, "I love you," every chance you get, because you never know when it will be the last time that you'll speak to them or see them again.

Love always and forever

Contents

Acknowledgments. vii

1. Born into Royalty 1
2. Growing up Fast. 7
3. The Crew 17
4. We Lost a Legend in '03. 21
5. Confessions of the Crew 25
6. It's a Crazy World. 29
7. Meeting the Men 35
8. Two Months Later 39
9. The Secret's Out 45
10. Miami Stay in Jersey 51
11. Separating from the Crew 61
12. Meeting His Mom 67
13. Decisions 73
14. The Aftermath. 81
15. Rude Awakening 91
16. Leaving New Jersey 97
17. We Gotta Make It Work. 101
18. Too Good to Be True 107

19. Problems 119
20. New Shit 125
21. Boom 131
22. Back in Jersey 137
23. Still in Love 145
24. Getting Things Lined Up 155
25. Talking to God 163
26. Letters to Jerri 169
27. Closing the Doors 175

Sunshine through Darkness preview

1. Opening New Doors 185

Acknowledgments

Thank you, God, for every experience that you bring me through while I am on this journey called life. My soul continues to grow; I love you Lord. I want to thank all of my friends and family who purchase this book just because you love and believe in me. Special thanks to Kevin Carrington and Ilda "Dania" Njango for the long nights of listening and editing. You two gave me the confidence to believe in my project. I don't know what I would have done without you, Kevin. Thank you so much. I am so blessed to have a friend like you. You're the best! Thanks to everyone at TECSKY Affiliates for believing in my project and giving me a chance. Latasha, Titika, Ebony and Jadona, I told you I would do it.

Special thanks to Grael Norton, Hayley Love and everyone at Wheatmark for all of your assistance. Kole Black thank you, I know that god sent you. Thanks to everyone at Weather Da Storm Entertainment for all of your support. An addition I want to thank Albie at Cheddar Magazine DVD and Marvin Walker at Elese Entertainment. I would also like to thank *you*, the person reading this, because you took the time to buy this book and read it. Thank you, it means so much to me.

In addition, I want to thank Nancy Stevenson, Yolanda Shaw, Kevin Jennings, Karimeh Smith, Dre Kelly, Kyaysha

Weatherington, Nikki Rocker, and Chris McMillian. Thank you for being my friends—I love you all! Cory, Zack, Dog, and Rah Jack, love ya!

Thanks to Darryl "Jason" Wilson at Sony for saving my project; I could have killed you that day!

Special thanks to my daughters, Skylar Ariza and Raymondra Saffold; my parents, Elaine and Samuel Jones; my birth father, Tony Chester; my brothers, Tony Chester and Samuel Jones; my sister, Timakii Chester; my favorite aunt, Gazette Burke; my favorite cousin Lil Warren Freeman; and all of my friends and family—you know who you are. Thank you, I love you all!

Tonetta Chester

Chapter 1

Born into Royalty

Royalty. I was born into royalty. My family was hood rich for as long as I could remember. I never wanted for anything. My parents divorced when I was just three years old, and my father never did shit for us. My mother, on the other hand, strove to provide the best life she could for my brother and me, by any means necessary. My mother, Jackie Harris—also known as "Red" because of her skin tone—was a true hustler. She was born to hustle, and getting money was her thing. She was introduced to the dope game by her older brother, L. J. The two of them worked together as a team, and in no time, the entire family—except for me—was in on all the deals.

They had the city of Miami on lock. They provided cocaine to everyone—and I mean *everyone*. They didn't fuck with the Columbians—everyone thought the Columbians ran Miami, but my family ran a larger portion of the city. It was my mother's job to import the cocaine directly from the distributor, who just happened to be her lover. My mother would bring the cocaine in from the Bahamas on her boyfriend's private jet. It was the easiest and safest way to get the job done in the '80s, and my mother was the best at it.

The '80s were big money for my family, very big money. I'm talking millions. My uncle Mike made so much money that he built his dream home with cash. His house was over

11,000 square feet, with a five-car garage and an Olympic-size pool. It had two tennis courts and a basketball court. My uncle even had a live-in housekeeper. I loved going to his house. It was like heaven.

My mother was the family's best-kept secret. She didn't play any games; she was all business. But in 1990, her brother L. J. was set up by his best friend and business associate, Larry. Larry and one of his friends planned to rob and kill my uncle. They were successful; Uncle L. J. was pronounced dead on the scene—and so was Larry. That's what happens when you take chances. Larry set up my uncles and didn't realize that he was being set up at the same time. My mother was deeply saddened; she would visit the spot where my uncle was killed on a weekly basis. It took her a while to accept the death of Uncle L. J. They were close, very close.

So much went wrong that year. My mother's best friend, Sharon, was picked up at the airport by the DEA. She was caught carrying five kilos of cocaine. After a lengthy trial, she was sentenced to twenty-five years in a federal penitentiary. It was a crazy year, but my mom couldn't allow her family to lose the street credibility that she and her brother had worked so hard for. She continued to work vigorously to maintain the lifestyle that she had become accustomed to, but with all the tragedy around her, she began to use the very drugs that she sold.

She kept her drug habit under control, not allowing it to affect her business. My mother used drugs as an escape from the life that she began to hate. When Annie, Mom's closest cousin, lost her battle with AIDS, my mother began to reevaluate her life. She didn't stop dealing; she just made better choices. She decided to take some time off and focus on my brother and me, leaving the operation for her younger brothers, Bert and Mike, to run.

They made the family more money than ever by tapping into new markets. They began to move weight from Florida to the Carolinas. There was nothing stopping them. They even incorporated the younger generation to help put the weight on the road. The '90s looked like they were going to be better then the late '80s, but that came to an end quickly in1991. My uncle Sed got caught on the road with work that he was carrying for Uncle Mike. If he would have just listened to his mother … She told him not to do it, but he did it anyway. The State charged him with trafficking cocaine, and he was sentenced to seven years and six months. He kept his mouth shut and did his time. He was replaced by a new runner within days. That's just how the game goes.

The family had another good year, but again, in 1993, another runner got caught. But this time it wasn't the State; it was the Feds. It was said that Cousin Fred didn't hold things down like Uncle Sed, but who knows? All I know is the Feds began to watch our family. They said it was because of Uncle Bert's flamboyant lifestyle. He owned a million-dollar home and a Rolls-Royce to go with it. He lived for attention and his ghetto-fabulous lifestyle made him one of America's Most Wanted. I'll never forget the day that the show aired—it was July 3, 1992. My uncle was the last person to be broadcasted. Uncle Bert had his hand in *all* of the cookie jars. He was wanted for bank fraud. He stole over eight hundred thousand dollars from an FDIC bank and the Feds wanted him bad. They showed his house, his cars, and all types of pictures. They stated that he was armed and dangerous and a charming con man. That had me confused—an armed and dangerous, charming con man? That was funny. Uncle Bert owned a house directly across the street from my grandmother, so everyone in the neighborhood knew exactly who he was. My grandmother was so embarrassed that she didn't go out-side for weeks. Eventually, the press died down and things got back to normal—almost. That winter, my mother won $578,000 on a lottery ticket, and. everyone was so excited that they forgot about Bert's TV appearance.

It was time for my mother to get back to work, but things had changed. So many of my mother business associates were in jail and to make matters worse, it was an election year, so the government was coming down heavy on the dope game and all its players. It wasn't like the '80s any-more; it was 1994. You couldn't just hop on a boat or jet at the port; the DEA would stop loads on the regular. My mother wasn't sure that she was ready to fill her old shoes. She hadn't touched any major work in about three years. My father had died in 1993, so she was collecting about forty-seven hundred dollars each month from Social Secu-rity. Since my mother was my father's last legal wife, she was able to collect Social Security along with the money for my brother and I. Unknown to my mother, my father was at General Contractor, making over seventy thousand dollars a year. Our Social Security check was the most he ever did for us. It took his death for him to finally to take care of his kids. My mother still had some change left over from the lottery; therefore, she didn't really need to hustle. I think the lifestyle just excited her, but that excitement ended when the school called home to tell my mother that my brother was caught selling weed at school. She went crazy; my mother had worked so hard to give us the best. I guess she didn't realize the impact of the lifestyle that she had opened our eyes to. We were fully aware of every-thing; we knew where she kept the scale, tape, roach spray, plastic wrap, and even the black spray paint. We knew of all the things that went on in our garage, and my brother was at that age where he wanted to be a part of the crew.

Being faced with that new reality, my mother decided to let go of the game. It was hard, I think, but my brother and I was more important to her. She didn't realize it was too late; my brother was already gone.

It took the Feds three and a half years to catch Uncle Bert. But they finally got their man. After the indictments, things started getting rough. Everyone knew that Feds were watching our family, and people kept their distance. However, James, one of my mother's good friends, continued buying from the family. His team was supplying a major part of the Midwest. He was one of the family's most valued customers, but the Feds were watching him too. Eventually, James's entire operation was shut down and the Feds indicted the whole crew. A total of thirteen people were involved; six of them were James brothers, three of his nephews and four of his cousins. They were indicted on conspiracy charges. Conspiracy basically meant that someone was tipping off the FBI. My mother and James had a real close relationship, so the whole family attended the trial. It was awful. The Feds moved their trail to northern Florida, and the jurors were all white.

What happened to a jury of your peers?

There was no way that they would win this trial. We stayed in Jasper, Florida, for one week while the trial went on. That Friday, after the closing arguments, it only took the jury one hour to come back with the verdict: *Guilty as charged!* James was sentenced to thirty-three years; one guy in their crew got ninety-nine years; another got forty-two. I wrote it all down — "33, 99, 42, 28, 41, 38, 30, 35, 32, 40, 32, 31, 31" — and added it up: 512 years!

Chapter 2

Growing up Fast

While my brother, Rob, was going through his "need to be a dope boy" stage, I guess I needed a father figure. I was just sixteen when I got pregnant from a twenty-five-year-old sexual predator. When my mother found out, she sent me away to Atlanta, Georgia. No one knew of my pregnancy until I returned a year later with the child that I was supposed to have put up for adoption. When I returned home, things were different. My mother had gotten married while I was gone; I had a stepfather and a five-year-old little brother. It was all new to me; I didn't like my new stepfather or the little badass boy. I just wanted out of their house. I hated my mother for what she had pulled at the hospital in Georgia, when she came to my room—while I was in labor—and said that she wished that my daughter would be born dead. I will never understand what I did to her to make her feel that way. I just knew that I hated her and I wanted out—I guess you can say I wanted to be grown. My mom required only a high school diploma to move out of the house, so when I graduated in June of 1999, I packed my things, and my daughter and I moved out immediately. After a bad relationship with Don, my high school boyfriend, I began to date a professional athlete in 1999. I had known him for a few years; we'd attended the same high school. Our relationship was good, but he was ready for marriage and the whole nine yards. I was still just eighteen and still trying to have a little fun. I wasn't ready to be some housewife, waiting at home while he was traveling from city to city doing his thing. So when he went back to California to play ball, I closed the door on our relationship; it was time to move on.

It was a new chapter in the family business; shit was back and popping. My uncle Sed had been released in May of 1999. He spent that year lining his soldiers up. It was time for the new generation to take over the family business. My brother had been waiting for this opportunity for years, and my uncle Sed gave it to him. Being a part of the team was about heart, trust, and teamwork. My uncle selected a few of my cousins—the ones that he thought were ready to take on the role. I was surely not selected. My uncle gave me the title "white girl" early on. I wasn't with the bullshit. I didn't take chances for anyone. They say I was selfish like my father; I say they were crazy. I seen enough niggas go to jail to know I didn't want any part of the streets. And besides, I had a daughter to live for.

The drought was over. The younger generation had brought street credibility back to the family's name in less than one year. My uncle Sed was the king of Miami, and my brother was his right hand. They had one motive: to get money. These niggas were true fools, and the party scene was their spot. They did everything extra. My uncle owned several businesses, including an independent record label call DES entertainment.

In 2000, I decided it was time to buy a house. I had a mortgage and a car payment all at the tender age of nineteen. I worked hard for everything I owned; I attended a local college and worked full-time to keep the bills paid.

That year I met Christopher Mathis. He was young, but he was nice. We met on South Beach. I was shopping, and he was hanging out with friends. We played the phone thing for a while, and we grew to be good friends. I would call him when I was bored, and he would call me in between classes. One time, I just happened to called him when we were both in Orlando. I was taking my daughter to Disney World for her birthday, and he was attending the Orlando Football Classic. We were just eight miles apart, so we met up at the Hard Rock Cafe inside of Universal CityWalk. Damn, I didn't know he looked so good. It was his birthday, October 29, so I gave him a birthday hug and kiss. At that moment, we promised to call each other more often. I decided to keep him in my back pocket—he had potential. Not only was he good-looking, he was also a senior at Florida A&M, majoring in business.

The next weekend, he was in Miami baking me a cake. We spoke of his plan to move back to Miami after he graduated from school. He planned to work with his father, Marvin Mathis. Mr. Mathis owned a well-respected engineering firm with seven locations across the United States. His family was well connected in the political scene in Miami. They were different from what I was used to.

We spent the next year in a long-distance relationship. We traveled back and forth between Tallahassee and Miami every weekend. We partied our asses off most of the time. I never really got into hanging out until I started dating him. I had my daughter when I was young, so clubbing was never on my to-do list. In fact, I never drank alcohol. I was a bona fide good girl, and I just got caught up with the baby thing. We had so much fun in Tallahassee. Christopher, Dimp, and Kenny promoted club parties in Tallahassee. In fact, they promoted the most popular events. Dimp was a local radio DJ; so Christopher and I was always VIPs. I had the time of my life that year. I met so many people, so many different celebrities; we hung out with everybody. I always looked forward to Dimp week. This was a week of parting for Dimp's birthday. I finally had the opportunity to see what I was missing out on—the whole college lifestyle. I'm a full-time student, but I attended evening classes with working professionals at the local college. It was not at all like being in a college town full of young people having fun.

The following summer, he moved into my place. It was a crazy summer; Christopher's father decided to tell his fiancée of four years that he was going to marry his mistress, Karen—who just happened to be my cousin's baby momma. It was a complete surprise to me that his mistress was *that* Karen. Here's a powerful black business man at the top of his game, fooling around with a ho, a real ho. She had four kids, all from different men. This had to be a joke! The family bashing came quickly; when she found out that Christopher and I was dating, we found out that our families hated each other! I never really knew why. All I know is after my cousin and Karen's relationship ended, our families never spoke. It was a mess. I wasn't going to say a word about her and the fact that she come from a generation of hos. Her grandmother still worked at the strip club as a bartender.

Karen told Christopher's father that my family was dangerous. She said that my family ran a drug cartel and that Christopher should stay away from us. Little did she know it was too late to ruin our relationship; Christopher and I was closer than most people knew. She tried so hard to keep us apart. She came up with more and more stories, and finally I was banned from Christopher's father's house. The ban only lasted a few weeks, because none of her stories made any sense. Remember, I was a good girl and I played the role well. Her stories just didn't add up, even if there was an inkling of truth! Karen and Mr. Mathis married that summer. She and I both came to an under-standing that we're not going anywhere, so we just needed to respect each other.

Christopher and I did the family thing for about a year—I guess you can say we played house—and it was great un-til Christopher decided that he was going to quit working for his dad and become a Realtor. He suggested I go back to school to become a mortgage broker so we could be a team. I didn't bite; I was comfortable getting a paycheck every two weeks. But I supported him; I was a team player. Supporting him meant that I would cover most of the bills by myself for a couple months, and that was fine. Until we went out with Mr. McKnee. Kenny McKnee was a close friend of Christopher's. You would have thought he was a millionaire—he was arrogant as hell. Most people didn't like him. I just learned how to accept him. I knew he'd be around forever, and since I planned to be with Christopher for the rest of my life, I knew Kenny would be a part of our family.

Who would have ever known that one day Kenny would cause the end of our relationship? The three of us went out for brunch, but unfortunately our order came out wrong. I didn't realize how angry the waitress at the Cheesecake Factory made me. That's probably what caused me to over-react and engage in the childish argument that sparked the beginning of the end for me and Christopher.

Kenny has the type of personality that will force your hand if you let his comedic wit get to you—which brings us to Christopher's eviction notice. It all came to a head when Christopher started to make jokes about Kenny's ri-diculous caking habits. You see, Kenny is the type of guy you want to hook your best friend or your sister up with because he spends and spends and spends money on his girls. It's like there's no end to his caking. He would try so hard to make you think that he was a millionaire. He would max his cards out trying to impress chicks.

Let me get back on track. Kenny and Christopher was going back and forth about his caking habits, and, me being the nosy girl that I am, I decided to add my two cents ... Okay, okay. Maybe I added a dollar. I simply pointed out to Christopher that maybe he should start pulling his own weight.

Let me fill you guys in: As you already know, Christopher and I was living together at this time, and his "going back to school" venture was getting a little carried away. He was getting away with murder; he wasn't paying any bills and he got way too comfortable. And since the topic of women and money was on the table, I saw the perfect opportunity to raise the rent on my tenant. It started off very "ha ha ha" but quickly became a "he he hell" as we went back and forth about the subject.

He was crying, "It ain't my place, I don't own it. Why should I pay the mortgage?" and I was saying what any rational human being would say, "You eat, sleep, and shit here, so why shouldn't you?" All the while, Kenny is steadily adding the occasional, "You gonna let her talk to you like that?" or "Wow, you gonna let him just let you pay all the bills while he eats up all the food?" It was inevitable; tension began to heighten, and I was starting to see things clearer and clearer—Christopher Mathis was a freeloader. I couldn't believe I had put up with this, so I said what any strong, independent black woman with a deadbeat boyfriend should say: "Get your shit and leave! Your instigating-ass homeboy's truck is outside, so it should only take you one trip to move back into that small-ass room in your daddy's house," and that's what ended our relationship. You may think I took it too far, but I'm a loyal chick and very private for that matter. I felt so disrespected; why would Christopher be debating with Kenny about *our* personal business? There I was, standing tall, holding things down, and he gonna front on me! We shared so many things and went through so much after our ectopic pregnancy. I just knew that we would be together for life. How could he dare disrespect me? He let pride get in his way, and I let pride help him pack. I was so heartbroken that day. But I couldn't take that attitude.

Besides, my uncle wasn't going to help me get the new C230 Mercedes Benz if I had a boyfriend. I really wanted the new Benz; it was smooth and sexy and I just had to have it. I knew my uncle wasn't going to help me get it if I had a nigga. My uncle and brother believed that men were supposed to take care of the house, so as long as you had a nigga, you couldn't really get much out of my uncle or my brother. They didn't realize that everyone didn't have it like them. As much as a nigga wanted to take care of his home, sometimes a nigga just didn't have money to waste. I didn't sympathize with guys , but I understood that everyone didn't have like us. I debated that point with my uncle once, and he told me, "If you choose to settle for a nigga that's just ain't got it, that your choice."

Consequently, I got my Benz that summer, a few months after I end my relationship with Christopher. The single life got played out fast. Most niggas didn't holla at me; that had a lot to do with my family. I'll never forget—I was on a date when I received a phone call from my brother instructing me to leave. I could never figure out how he knew where I was and who I was with. More so, who the hell did he think he was? He shared the same name as our father, but our father was dead. And who listened to him anyway? He called me back ten minutes later: "You didn't leave yet. Get from around that corny-ass nigga." I scanned the room and didn't see any familiar faces; my brother couldn't have known him. I only date professional men, so I was puzzled. I wasn't going to allow him to ruin my night, so I pressed the power-off button on my cell phone and enjoyed my dinner. When I arrived home, my brother was there with a few choice words for me: "You need to start listening. Don't talk to that nigga—and if he has your number, change it."

"What?" I screamed.

"You heard me," he said.

"Boy, whatever."

"You better listen, girl. Where did you meet him?"

"On the beach. Why?"

"What did he tell you he do?"

"What the fuck is going on; do you know him or something?"

"Just answer me."

"I met him on South Beach. He owns a chain of barbershops throughout the state, about eleven. Why? Tell me what's going on."

"You still don't let niggas pick you up from the house, right?"

"Right."

"You be checking your mirror; nobody followed you?"

I always check my rearview mirror to see if anyone is following me, and he knew it. I said, "Look, I'm on top of my game. Nobody comes to my house, and nobody can follow me. I'm on point with my mirror game. Tell me what's going on."

"Okay. I took something from that nigga. I know his soft ass very well. I don't know if he trying to be slick by talking to you, but don't fuck with him. I don't know his intentions. Did he ask about me?"

"No, he didn't. So how did you know I was with him?"

"I have some people on him. They called and said you

got out of his car with him, in front of Club Bed around 9:30. He had a dinner reservation for two. You ordered lobster and he ordered rosemary chicken, right?"

"Damn, were they sitting next to us?"

"No, fool. Just stop talking to that nigga. I gotta go; I got some business to take care of."

"I need some money."

"You always begging bitch."

"I got your bitch, nigga." I watched him count off ten twenty-dollar bills from his wad. "Thanks, love ya," I said, smiling.

Chapter 3

The Crew

I couldn't help but notice the full moon; it was a lovely night. I was leaving Club Bed on South Beach when this dude tapped on the window of my uncle's Mercedes–Benz S 600. I recalled seeing the dude in the club earlier that night; he was with a gang of niggas. I could tell that they were not from Miami, but who is? I noticed him when he jumped out of the black Hummer limousine in front of me, but I was too busy trying to change the radio station to care who he was or where he was going. Therefore, I didn't notice that he was standing at the window of the car until he tapped. He startled me; it was Friday the thirteenth. I was a little hesitant, but I went ahead and rolled down the window.

"What's up, Ma? What you doing tonight?"

"Nothing. I'm just going home."

"Home? It's still early. Me and my boys are having a party in our room tonight; we're staying at the Loews on Collins and Seventeenth Street. You should follow us there."

He went on and on; his lips kept moving, but I was busy looking at the rest of the crew. I was not listening, especially after he hit me with the 'room party' line. Who does this dude think he's talking to? I quickly cut him off.

"Call me tomorrow, 305-610-1910. My name is Neshela, and by the way, I don't do room parties! Don't try me again, nigga." I pulled off, not giving him a chance to say a word.

"Ay, my name is Wesley."

The next day he called. I noticed an unusual number when I looked at the caller ID, but I answered it anyway. "Hello?"

"Hey, this is Wesley. We met last night in front of the club."

"Oh, hey. Where is 973?"

"New Jersey, Ma."

"Oh. Okay Mr. New Jersey, What up?"

"Nothing really. Me and my boys are getting ready to go to Aventura Mall. You should meet us out there."

"That's cool, give me an hour I'll meet y'all up there."

When I arrived at the mall two hours later, Wesley and his crew was getting ready to leave. Wesley wanted to go to a more urban mall, so I took him to Pembroke Lakes Mall. He picked up a few sneakers, and we headed back to the beach. He's a cool dude, aside from the fact that he isn't my type. I spent most of the day driving this nigga around and he didn't even offer me any gas money. I didn't need the gas; it was the fact that he didn't offer—that quickly makes him not my type!

That evening, I hung out with Wesley and his crew. They were all from New Jersey; they called themselves the NJ Boyz. They are definitely hot—even the do boys looked good. They were different from Miami niggas; they had their own swagger. We went out to Club Opium on South Beach. These Jersey boys sure knew how to party. Bottles after bottles, they kept them coming. I just watched. I don't drink; my mother taught me that all niggas have hidden agendas, and it is best to be on top of your game at all times. That's why drinking or smoking has never been my thing. I have never tried either of them. We ended the show at 4:00 AM. I was so tired; I had to be up for work at 6:30 AM. The following weekend, the Jersey boys came back to Miami and we had a ball.

The crew stayed in Miami on a regular basis. Miami was like their second home. They came down every other weekend, usually Friday until Monday. We partied our asses off that summer. I barely went out with my family anymore; I would just plan my partying around their trips to Miami. After hanging out with these fools, I didn't have time to hang out with anyone else. Our party schedule was as follows: Friday night we go to Club Bed; Saturday, the Waffle House and the mall. We never go out on Saturday night; everybody does their bitch thing—you know, fucking the chick they met the night before. On Sunday night, we hang out at Opium, and we party our asses off. I remember one night, a few of us were hungry, and the waitress at Opium had five boxes of pizza delivered to our VIP section. Opium didn't serve food, so that made us the center of attention. We were off the chain.

It took me a minute to figure out the position each nigga plays in the crew, mostly because my vision was clouded by Wesley. He made it seem like he was the man, always talking about his open cases and his million-dollar lawyer. At first I really thought he was the man, but in due time I found out that he is just the hype man. You can read everything about Wesley in seconds. I wasn't paying attention, so I just didn't notice. Don't get me wrong—he did his thing, but not the way he led me to believe. There was a few more crew members like him, but no one was as hype as Wesley. Wesley is a true clown—very funny. He told me everybody's business, and I listened. We became cool over time. He is my nigga. Not my man, but my nigga.

Here is the way it went: I met Wesley in the summer of 2002; he then introduced me to his crew—well, I should say *the* crew, because he didn't run shit but his mouth. After the first couple of trips to Miami, he tried to fuck me, but my period was on. So then he suggests that we have anal sex. I'm not with that gay shit, so nothing went down. Then, on another trip—I happened to be in Jersey this time—and again he tried to get some, but his dick wouldn't get hard. At least that's what I thought at first. He tried me with that anal shit again! And you already know, *I'm not with that gay shit*! That's when I realized that his dick was only one and a half, okay, maybe two inches, so then it all made sense. He liked anal sex because he could inflict pleasure during anal intercourse. He couldn't work the middle with his little-ass dick. I have never in my life seen a grown-ass man with a dick that small, and I'm not joking! From that day forward, we both knew that there couldn't be shit between us. That's why Wesley was always just my nigga. We talked like two bitches; he was a gossiping-ass nigga. Talking to Wesley was better than talking to any of my homegirls.

Chapter 4

We Lost a Legend in '03

John's home. It was the last week of August in 2003 when John was released from jail. He was one of my uncle's nigga team members. He did most of the dirty work, most of the murders. He was arrested a year earlier for attempted murder, but because of a technicality they'd had to release him. Those niggas partied their asses off that week. It's a celebration; everyone was happy to have John back.

I was lying in my bed half asleep when the ghost called. I refer to him as the ghost because no one even knew that we conversed—we were having a secret affair. He called to inform me that my uncle Sed had been shot. I thought I was dreaming. It was the second day of September, one year earlier, when the ghost had called to tell me that my brother had been shot in the head and was being airlifted to Jackson Memorial Hospital. It was a miracle that my brother lived. The bullet was just three centimeters from his brain. This year it was my uncle. I had just talked to him that morning. We were all together on Tuesday night at the Improv Comedy Club in Coconut Grove. I was pulling out of the parking garage when I'd noticed my brother and uncle walking toward Club Oxygen. I yelled out the window to my uncle, asking for money, as usual.

"Damn, bitch. You always begging. I just bought you this Benz." He had a way of making you feel ungrateful, but I was used to it, so it didn't bother me at all. I knew someone was going to get the money.

"Un, you didn't buy me this Benz; I have a car note. But thanks for the down payment! Anyway, that was like a month ago. Come on, Un. I'm broke."

"Okay white girl, you want some money? Come hang out with the crew. We ain't gon' to be waiting at the door for you all night." He probably thought I wasn't going to bother coming to the club, knowing I was pulling out of the parking garage. Plus, he knew I hated when they called me white girl, but I surprised them all. I parked my car and walked in the club.

"We was just about to leave you outside," my uncle teased.

"Whatever. Let's party." We're supposed be celebrating John's homecoming, but he didn't show up. He was too busy trying to make a baby.

Damn, what could have happened?

"Neshela, Neshela, can you hear me?" the ghost shouted. "Your uncle just got shot up on Biscayne and Forty-first Street. It's two bodies! We don't know who was with him. *Get up now!*" I hung up the phone and called my uncle—no answer. I immediately called my brother—no answer.

What could have happened? Where are they?

After the ghost called, my phone didn't stop ringing. The tears began to roll from my eyes. As I wiped my face, I called my cousin Jamal to inform him of the news; he was already on the road, heading to the crime scene.

I hopped on the turnpike, headed to the city. As I look at the stars above, all I could do was pray. When I arrived at the scene, I walked right into the ghost. He wanted to console me but he couldn't. People were everywhere; it was like a fucking parade. Everyone was there, including my uncle's host of whores.

The Metro-Dade police had to block the street to contain the crowd. This misdeed took place at a high-profile basketball player's barbershop. For that reason, the local media was all over the story.

When my brother showed up, my mother and I sighed with some relief, but we were still worried. There was no word from my uncle. It had been hours and no word yet; we were there all night, watching and waiting. We had no clue as to what bodies lay beneath the sheets. No matter what position or title you carried, we all shared the same pain the night.

My brother, uncles, and cousins replayed the day over and over again. That afternoon, they'd all attended little Sed's football game in Miami Lake. After the game, my uncle stopped by his studio to check on an artist. Later that day, John and my uncle headed to the barbershop to get fresh for the evening. It was a big night; my uncle was closing a deal for a club on South Beach. But he never made it.

That fall, after my uncle was killed, the crew was indicted. It was like winter in Miami—everything was at a standstill. Shit was crazy. Niggas had DES tagged all over the place and the local radio station 99 Jamz played "I Miss You" by Strawberry and Trick Daddy. This song was dedicated to my uncle and his memory. The family drama got sick; you wouldn't believe the stories if I told you. All I know is it was getting cold in New Jersey, and so the NJ Boyz stayed in Miami. We became like family over the years, and every time Jersey was in Miami, I was there. They became my outlet for fun and partying. Wesley, Quan, Jack, Mack, Dog, Blue—the whole crew. Quan and I became close. For some reason, he reminded me of my uncle, and Mimi, his girlfriend, was like the sister I never had.

Chapter 5

Confessions of the Crew

One weekend when the crew was in town, Wesley and I listened to "Burn," by Usher, over and over again. Mimi and Quan pleaded with us to turn it off. I was just like that with music—I could listen to one song all day. I don't think anyone could forget Usher's CD *Confessions*, especially not Mack; he was going through his own confession. Not only did he live the song a year earlier, he seemed to never know who he wanted to be with. One weekend, Mack and I was shopping for purses for his girl-on-the-side, Tammy; the next weekend he was buying an engagement ring for Rochelle, his long-term girlfriend who he had been with for over seven years. She had just found out that Tammy was three months pregnant. I guess he thought proposing was the perfect plan to get his girl back. Tammy and Quan's girlfriend, Mimi, was best friends. In fact, Tammy and Mack hooked Quan and Mimi up. It was an interesting circle; the crew was crazy and always full of surprises.

It was finally time for me to take a vacation. My flight landed in Jersey around 2:30 PM on Friday, Quan and Jack picked me up from the airport, and we met the rest of the crew at John's Place for a late lunch. After lunch we rode around the city for a minute, then we headed to the house. We had a long night ahead of us; the NJ Boyz were having a party at Club Deco. My girlfriend Liz even flew into town for the event.

I had been to Jersey several times, but this was the first time that I partied with the crew in their city. It was finally time to go to the club, but Mimi was taking forever to get dressed, so we left her. Mimi was the slowest person in the world. I never met anyone that took so long to get dressed. I'm one of those fifteen-minute chicks; I can get dressed in fifteen to twenty minutes, tops. I don't wear makeup and I always keep it simple. I'm one of those naturally pretty girls, so I never understood why chicks take so long to get dressed. Mimi was the worst; she would make you change your mind about going out.

Finally, we made it to Club Deco! It felt like we were driving forever. We arrived at the club around midnight, and it was bananas. The club was roped off. It appeared as if the cops weren't letting anyone else in the club, but Quan drove up to the barricade anyway. He nodded his head at the cop; the cop nodded back. As he moved the barricade, we pulled straight up to the door and hopped out of Quan's black Range Rover. We walked around the metal detector and directly in the club. I was puzzled; I had never seen a metal detector in front of a club—a real metal detector, like the ones at the airport—and even more puzzling, we just walked around it. *What kind of shit is this?*

I was ready to party. I hadn't been out in a few months, since the death of my uncle, and it was finally time to relax and have fun. The crew was doing it. They had their own private VIP section with a bar, bartender, and bouncer. I had a ball that night. These niggas was Making It Rain way before Fat Joe and Lil Wayne. I couldn't help but think of my family and the fun that everyone used to have. I missed my uncle more than ever that night.

When I returned to Miami, I was informed that my un-

cle's crew was indicted over the weekend while I was partying my ass off in New Jersey. The doors were being kicked
in. The Feds picked up a total of 136 people, and my dead
uncle's name was at the top of the page. Shit was crazy. The
streets were dead, and even though I just got back in town,
I decided it was time for another trip to Jersey.

New Jersey was like my new escape. It became my new
vacation spot, and Mimi and I turned out to be good friends.
We were both Geminis, so we understood a lot about each
other. Prior to meeting Mimi, I heard lots of stories about
her, and when we first met a few years earlier she came
off a little extra. But she turned out to be cool as hell. We
talked on a daily basis, and Quan and I talked regularly
too. Over the next few years, we grow close. We shared our
stories, both good and bad. We were always there for each
other. I would just go to Jersey for the weekend just to chill
and get away.

Wesley and I was still cool—we just didn't really talk that
much. For some reason, no one was feeling Mimi. It was all
over some stupid shit. Mimi had her ways, but at the end
of the day she was a loyal friend to the people that she was
close to. Sometimes I would feel uncomfortable around the
rest of the crew. I understood both sides, but it was just one
of those things.

I remember I was in a similar situation once. I told my
cousin that I seen his girl—Karen—at the club with another
nigga, and when she got home he whipped her ass so bad
that they had to take her to the hospital. After everything
went down, he told her that it was me that told. She never
spoke to me again, and I couldn't blame her. I swore that I
would never involve myself in no one else's business. The
funniest part of it all was that they stayed together for a
while.

Chapter 6

It's a Crazy World

Just when we thought everything was going to be all right, in 2004, my brother and my nephew was leaving our mother's house when an unusual car began to follow them. He noticed earlier, while outside talking to our mother, that the same car had passed by. My brother was almost killed two years earlier during an attempted robbery. I guess you could understand why he was a little worried, especially with his two-year-old son in the car. Like any frightened father, he pressed the gas and hoped for the best. As it turned out, the unfamiliar car was a police detective driving an unmarked car, and you already know what happens when you run from the police. Yep, the helicopter, ten additional polices, and the top story on the six o'clock news that evening. *Here we go again!* And to make matters worse, my brother's long-term girlfriend was seven months pregnant. He received a slew of charges, ranging from child neglect to battery on a law enforcement officer.

His bond was only six hundred thousand dollars. Of course, we had a family bond man on call, but when we went to pick up my brother, there was a federal hold. My brother was indicted on gun charges, and so was my best friend, Lisa . She just happened to be my brother's ex-girlfriend. Lisa and I had been friends for about seven years.

We been through so much shit together. I'll never forget how our dumb asses didn't pass the HSCT to graduate from high school. We had to take the test twice; we even had someone steal the test so that we could study. I remember when I first bought my house. It was a foreclosure property that had been vacant for over a year. Lisa and I did everything; we were the painters, the movers, the handyman, the pest control—we did it all. We had our share of good times.

The funniest shit happened back in 1999. It was with my on-and-off-again boyfriend from high school, Don. He was at the house and another dude showed up. I was missing in action when it all started to go down, but when it was over, Lisa had to stand in the paint—I mean *literally* stand in the paint. Don and this other guy got into a fight. So Don decided to throw a bucket of paint at the dude's car. When I arrived Don decided to throw what was left of the paint on me Lisa just happened to be in the way.

There were bad times too, like when she had a problem with how close her boyfriend Stephen and I was. And when Stephen was killed, and she was two months pregnant with the child she chose not to keep—that was difficult. We had been through all of these things and more, but at the time she needed me the most, I couldn't be there for her. She made a deal with the Feds to talk against my brother. Inside, I understood; she was just twenty-three, facing thirty years for her involvement in one—or should I say eight brainless events.

It was definitely time for another vacation. I boarded a flight to Newark; I needed to escape the chaos in Miami. Quan picked me up from the airport and we went directly to the club. This time Wesley was having a party at some club in Linden. The club was nice, and of course the NJ Boyz had a separate VIP section upstairs, but shit got crazy.

Mimi and Rochelle began to beef at some point, from my understanding. Mimi would always see Mack hanging out with Rochelle while he was with still with Tammy so, like a friend, Mimi began to tell Tammy of Mack's actions. The average chick would have taken heed of the information and used it to her advantage, but Tammy wasn't strong enough to keep her sources confidential. She was five months pregnant, and it hurt her to hear that the woman she had played second to for so many years was possibly taking her place back. Tammy didn't want that to happen; therefore, she had to validate her story and give up her source—whatever it took to stay in the number one spot. What Tammy didn't realize was the tension that she brought between everyone when she admitted that Mimi was the one that told her everything. The craziest part of it all was that by then, Mack had left Tammy in the midst of her pregnancy to be back with Rochelle.

This shit never really made any sense to me; the whole thing was just stupid. It went on for almost a year. Tammy's son was two months old. Anyway, we were all partying when Mimi came running up the stairs screaming, holding her face. Blood was everywhere, and people were trying to figure out what was going on. Everyone's asking, "What happened; what's going on?" "Mimi's bleeding!" "Oh my god!" "My sister!" There was only a few of us that stayed calm. I just happened to be sitting by the ice, so I took some to place on the wound on Mimi's face as Quan held and shielded her. After that, Quan, Mimi, Mimi's best friend, Rachel, and I walked out of the side door of the club, and it seemed as if everyone just appeared outside. They were going back and forth trying to figure the entire thing out. And out of nowhere, Mimi's sister jumped on Tammy.

"Bitch, it's your fault my sister got cut!"

Moments later, Wesley and the rest of the crew began

to fight with some other niggas in the club. Quan, Mimi, and I was heading to the hospital. When we arrived, Mimi checked in.

"Use my name, Neshela Jones," I whispered to her as we walked up.

When we got to see a doctor, he asked, "So what happened, Ms. Jones? Should we contact the police?"

"No, sir," Mimi said quietly.

"My name is Dr. Brown. I'll be fixing you up tonight. Don't worry, it's smaller than it seems; you'll be just fine."

As the tears rolled down her face, Mimi cried, "I can't model anymore! I'm going to kill that bitch."

The lobby began to echo; we could hear the whole crew. Everyone showed up to make sure she was good. Everyone but Tammy. In fact, Tammy left the club with Mack; she didn't even bother to call. As Denise and Nancy, Mimi's younger sisters, entered the room, I headed to the lobby feeling grateful and thanking God it was just a cut. In Miami, bitches had done stopped cutting each other. We had self-defense laws; even I owned gun. I never really heard of people fighting, but it seems that in Jersey, niggas and bitches got off on it.

It was time for me to take a break from New Jersey; shit was too crazy. Mack and Quan are two niggas of the same crew and their chicks couldn't get along. These bitches were going back and forth, jumping each other, keeping up a mess. I guess nobody had respect for their man or for themselves. These bitches were just overreacting. No one was thinking of the attention that they were attracting or how they made their man look in the streets.

It was New Year's when I finally took another trip back to Jersey. I only went because it was Quan's birthday, and Mimi had worked so hard to pull everything off that I had to be there. We had dinner at Bill's house. Afterward we took two limousines to Atlantic City. There, we celebrated Quan's birthday. It was an enjoyable evening and the weather was just right—right for our coats! But I couldn't enjoy the weather; I had to be in and out. Home was the safest place to be. Shit was hot up top. The NJ Boyz were feuding with some niggas from down the hill. I even slept with a nine millimeter under my pillow that night.

Chapter 7

Meeting the Men

It was Sunday, May 21, when I met J. I'll never forget the day; Mimi and I was supposed to go shopping, but instead, she had an appointment with one of the high-paying clients at her hair salon, who tipped well too. So you already know she canceled our shopping trip to twist hair. I was pissed! I had been in Jersey for over a week and was scheduled to leave the following day. We had spent most of our time shopping for house stuff; Mimi and Quan had just bought a new house, and Quan was tired of shopping with Mimi. As a result, he flew me up to do the dirty work. A week of shopping for house stuff with Mimi was crazy! She was always so indecisive.

All I know is that I wasn't about to give up my day to watch Mimi twist some nigga's hair. So I took Quan's daughter, Nicole, instead. We hopped in the CLK, pulled off Chancellor, and jumped on the parkway—Shore Hill, here we come! It wasn't like shopping with Mimi, Nicole is just sixteen. But she's not as picky or as talkative as Mimi, so I made the best of it.

Coincidentally, when we returned to the shop, Mimi's client was still there. I didn't even know him, but I didn't like him at all; I just looked at him. My homegirl opened her shop on Sunday just for him. *Who the hell do this nigga think he is?* That's all I could think. He was arrogant as hell, but I must admit he had swagger out of this world. We exchanged a few words while Mimi put the last twist in place. *Finally, time to leave.* Mimi had to drop Nicole off to her mom first and then meet one of her girlfriends at Fargo Salon.

We're in the car for just a few minutes when the phone rang. Mimi burst out laughing while handing the phone to me, "It's for you." Shockingly, it was Mimi's client, asking to take me to dinner. Considering I didn't know him, I called Quan to get the clear. After I received the clear from Quan, the dude agreed to pick me up from Fargo Salon on Bergen Street. He took me downtown to restaurant called Spain. He ordered shrimp scampi, and I don't even remember what I had. All I know is that I was sitting across the table from this nigga that was just amazing. He was wearing a pair of Roberto Cavalli shades, with a green, pink, and white Ralph Lauren polo. He wasn't the most attrac- tive dude, but he definitely had swagger—and style, for that matter.

It was something keeping me glued. He just knew he was the shit; he talked with a slur, pressing his teeth against his bottom lip. He was sexy as hell.

"So what is your name?" I asked him when we sat down.

"J. But you can call me J, Billy, Mr. Bowie, or whatever you like."

We talked over dinner for about an hour. He revealed that he met me two years earlier at Club Deco. I didn't remember meeting him, but I guess I shouldn't have. He didn't say a word to me that night. He just inquired about me. It blew my mind—he remembered the exact date and what I was wearing. I was flattered; he had a flashbulb memory of me from two years ago. But the night had to come to an end. I was leaving for Miami the following day, and he was attending family cruise to Jamaica.

My flight left Newark at 4:30 PM. I landed in Miami at 8:15 sharp. I was totally ecstatic and happy to be home; I drove straight there.

The first call came two days after we shared dinner. J informed me that he was in Miami, in route to Jamaica. Coincidentally, his cruise departed from the Port of Miami. He asked if I would meet him at the airport for a bite to eat. I wanted to but I couldn't; Miami International was too far for me to make it in time. He insisted that I could make it, as if he was the engine in my car. It was obvious that he was used to having things his way and *no* was not acceptable. He was in for a rude awakening—or maybe I was. He hung up in a rush, stating that he would call me when he got some free time—since I was too busy for him.

It was two and half weeks when I finally received the second call from J. I thought it was funny.

"I guess I'm on punishment or you were just too busy to call me, Ms. Lady!" he said.

"Are you crazy, boy? Last time we talked, you hung up, saying you would call me. So I guess I'm on punishment, or maybe you just got some free time!"

What J didn't understand about me was I wasn't the type to sweat or show interest. I was confident that he would call sooner or later—besides, he remembered me from two years ago.

We couldn't get enough of each other; I didn't understand how it all went down. For a month, we spent countless hours on the phone; we even slept on the phone. We talked about everything; there were no boundaries in our conversations. I received the nickname "Miami" early on. You see, Miami isn't just about partying and having fun. It's the spirit inside of you, the spirit that emerges when you're surrounded by the ocean breezes, the swaying palm trees, the rays of energy from the sun, and the beauty. I carry it all with me everywhere—my conversation, my walk, my smile, my style. It was all new to him; that why he called me Miami. You can never get enough of Miami; in fact, it keeps you coming back. If you ever been to Miami, you know what I'm talking about.

Chapter 8

Two Months Later

It was finally time. Two months after we met, I flew to New Jersey to see him. He picked me up from Newark International Airport around 3:00 PM on Friday. Angela, the driver, dropped us off to an awaiting car on Jerri's block, Alpine. We rode around for a minute so he could square things up. We had no plans on coming out for the weekend; after all Miami was in Jersey.

We spent the entire weekend in bed, talking and listening to my iPod, reminiscing on songs that had meaning to us. I was determined not to fuck him, and I didn't. But he didn't try me, so does that count? Over dinner, he finally disclosed his real name, Jerri Hopkins, and from that day forward that's the only name that I would call him. I wanted to be different; I refused to call him J, Billy, or Mr. Bowie. Jerri was original, like Neshela—one of a kind. I discovered so many things about Mr. Jerri Hopkins that weekend. He is just as arrogant as he came off when we first met, but I liked it. This dude didn't ever wear the same boxers or T-shirts twice, and he took everything to the cleaner's. There was no pots or pans—shit, there wasn't any food—at his house. He ate fast food for every meal.

I left Jersey Sunday, on flight number 234, and for the entire ride to the airport he played the first song that represented us, "Like You" by Bow Wow and Ciara. We would

sing the verses to each other, and we'd sing the chorus together:

I ain't neva had nobody show me all the things that you
done showed me
And the special way I feel when you hold me
We gon' always be together, baby, that's what you told
me
And I believe it ('cause I ain't neva had nobody do me
like u).

That was our song; music was our secret code of communicating. When we couldn't express how we felt, we
would play a song on each other's voice mail. Each song
represented us or a feeling that we had. You would have to
listen to each word to understand the meaning.

I was back in Jersey within days. To my surprise, he had
the entire weekend planned. He told me not to bring any
bags, and I didn't. Angela picked me up from the airport
and dropped me to an awaiting car on Jerri's block. We
spent most of the evening having dinner at Ruth's Chris.
When we got to his place, there were white rose petals
leading to his bedroom. I was taken by surprise; there were
bags everywhere, filled with stuff for me. Like a little girl
with new clothes, I tried everything on. I used his long
hallway as my catwalk and modeled each outfit, just for
him. There was a total of eighteen outfits, complete with
shoes and handbags. After my fashion show, he joined me
in the shower. As he washed my back, I opened my mouth
wide to let the water flow in. I love playing with the water
while in the shower, and apparently so did he.

When we awoke Saturday morning, we took our first
road trip. Atlantic City was our destination. "Never Been"
by Mary J Blige was the anthem song for the trip. I had

never heard the song prior to that day, but by the time we arrived in Atlantic City, I knew the whole song by heart. I had never been touched like this, kissed like this—or licked like this for that matter! Friday night, as we lay in the bed, our conversation was not at all like our usual chats. His lips began talking to my lips, not fast but slowly. He was very gentle, taking his time, not missing a spot. As he stucked my pussy, his tongue began to explore my ass as he flipped me over for a better position. I was so wet; I came over and over again. I begged him to stop; I began to scream, "Jerri, Jerri, stop! Please, J, please."

I had never experienced such treatment; I didn't know until that day what having my salad tossed meant. I was truly feeling Mary; I had never been ... Touched, licked, kissed, or fucked like this. We didn't speak much during the ride to Atlantic City; we were just caught up in the music, and I was still thinking of the night before.

As we pulled up to the Taj Mahal, he made one last call, promising there would be no interruptions as he pressed the power-off button on his cell. We were greeted by several employees as we entered the building. It was obvious that he was a regular guest at the Taj Mahal, and he was well respected. The hostess, whom he introduced as his aunt, escorted us to room 4033—the Grand Suite. The room was breathtaking (aside from its ocean view). The suite was decorated in pastel colors, with light-wood furnishings. It was over 1200 square feet, which included an oversized master bedroom with a Jacuzzi that was set off to the right of the room. To the left sat a 50-inch Panasonic flat-screen television. The bathroom was covered with marble; in the dining area, there was a larger stone table with four contemporary chairs. The suite also contained a parlor, powder room, and personal spa; the room was beautiful.

After getting settled, we decided to walk the pier. I ended

the walk quickly; I couldn't get used to the water. I had never seen water so misty gray; it was foggy and dirty. Being from Miami, I was used to seeing bright blue water with a green tint. When we returned to the room, I closed the blinds. I hated the look of the cloudy water—it was so depressing.

To my surprise, there was a box on the bed with my name on it. It contained a black Marc Jacobs dress with a pair of Gucci pumps. It was my dinner dress. We had dinner reservations for 7:00 PM at Dynasty, an oriental restaurant located in the Taj Mahal. We laughed and chitchatted over dinner, as usual. I enjoyed every moment of being with him. We were always overwhelmed with happiness, commanding attention from everyone around us. Talking was our favorite thing to do. I'm sure of that 'cause for the past two months, that was all we had, so that all we knew. Mak- ing love would soon become our new favorite thing to.That evening, he pressed my body against the marble tile that surrounded the shower. As the water beat against the small of his back, he gently kissed on my neck and his hand rubbed my mounds vigorously. It was not long before I could feel him inside of me. With every thrust, his silent breathing became more aggressive, and my body was very welcoming. He suddenly came to a dead stop. Even though I wasn't facing him, I could feel his eyes admire me from behind. Suddenly, he turned my body around, and the water began to beat on my face as he thrust me above his waistline. I could feel him entering my body again and again. To ensure I wouldn't fall, I wrapped both arms around his muscular neck and broad shoulders. I pulled myself in to him and relaxed to let him have his way with me as he bounced me up and down. It was the greatest sex I ever had. We didn't wake up till the following afternoon.

I drove us back to Newark; I had a flight to catch that

evening. When we arrived at Jerri's block to meet Angela, he introduced me to Malik, one of his niggas. Coincidentally, Malik had his chick in town from Atlanta, and they were also on the way to the airport. While we waited for Angela to arrive, Malik began chatting. I was hoping that he would remember his girl was sitting in the car in front of us, waiting on him to return. Malik was a little to extra for me. Angela pulled up right in time.

Chapter 9

The Secret's Out

We played the back-and-forth thing for a minute. I was back in Jersey the following weekend. There were no big plans this time, we just chilled. I arrived late on Friday, but we still made it to Ruth's Chris. Abdul, one of Jerri's close friends, joined us for dinner. He was like our third wheel. Abdul went to dinner with us all the time. He was cool as hell; I liked him from the door. He appeared to be a genuine friend to Jerri.

That weekend, I met up with Mimi for lunch. I guess it wasn't a good idea that I was keeping my trips to Jersey a secret. When I told Mimi of them, I had already been to Newark at least five times. I filled her in on the details—the trips to Atlantic City, the shopping, the sex—I told her everything.

She then informed me of the drama between Wesley and Jerri. She stated that she would have told me earlier if she had known that we were kicking it. I promised her that I wouldn't say a word unless Jerri brought it up. The crazy part about the whole thing is that I was still talking to Wesley on a regular basis. In fact, I had told him all about Jerri; I just never revealed his name. When Mimi told me of the pressing beef between them, I immediately stopped calling Wesley, and I avoided his calls for weeks. Wesley was completely unaware that Jerri and I had been fucking around for the past five months.

Wesley was my nigga; we talked about everything, and a part of me wanted to tell him earlier—I just knew he wasn't mature enough to hear it. Now that Jerri and I was always on the scene, I had to tell him. I didn't want to run into Wesley at John's Place, a popular soul food restaurant in Newark that we all liked, so finally, I decided to tell Wesley that I been dating J. I knew Wesley wouldn't be happy to hear this. I was back in Miami when it all went down.

Wesley called me and said, "What's up?"

"Shit," I answered.

"You up top this weekend?"

"Naw, nigga. I just got home yesterday, but I'll be back in Jersey tomorrow. Listen, I need to talk to you."

"What's up, Shela? You need something?"

"No, I'm good. Listen, you know my dude."

"That nigga that keep you in Jersey—you be up here acting like you don't know anybody," he complained.

"Listen, Wesley! I fuck with J."

"What J?"

"You know J. He knows you."

"You fuck with *that* nigga? He's a fucking bum! Come on Shela, that a setback, baby. I can't believe you fuck with that nigga." He laughed. "This shit is funny. Don't fuck him raw, yo."

"Damn, Wesley. You ain't gonna disrespect my dude like that! You know you my nigga, but respect me regardless of how you feel for him. I really like the dude, man."

"Shela, you're my girl but that nigga ain't shit. He's always trying to fuck with my bitches—he a wankster. Damn, so all this time you been back and forth, that the nigga you be with."

"Yes, that the nigga!"

"Shit, I'm fucking J-lo." He really thinks his girlfriend looks like J-lo. She is a cute girl. But if she's fucking him she can't be happy unless she's a virgin. Then he said, "I can't believe you fucking a bum. Damn, Shela, he's a backward-ass move for you; you too good for him. You know he be trying to fuck with Monique."

"Who is that?" I was well aware of who she was. She used to call Jerri all the time. He referred to her as his big sister, but he had informed me that he used to fuck her. Jerri made it seem like they just had a fuck thing. But Wesley spilled the beans differently.

"Remember that time you was up here at Mimi's shop and O-girl came to get my cell phone to put some music on it?"

"Okay, yeah, I remember. She was in a gold car, right?"

"Yeah, Monique. That's my girl; I used to fuck with her back in the day."

"You used to fuck Quan's baby mom?"

"Yeah, I was fucking her before she was his baby mom. But your nigga be sweating her."

"Really!"

"Yeah. Every time I'm with her, he be calling her; she don't even answer the phone. That nigga bought her a dia-mond watch."

"Shut up, Wesley."

"I'm for real. He be buying her all type of shit and he ain't even fucking her. This nigga was at her house and her dude came home. She had to hide him in the closet for two hours."

"Shut up, Wesley. You crazy."

"Shela, I'm serious. That nigga wack. You better get all you can, and don't fuck him raw, okay?"

"I hear you, fool. I'll talk to you later," I said, and I hung up. Wesley was always resourceful. It was just a few days later when Wesley called to fill me in with the entire story about Monique and Jerri's secret affair. He made it seem like Jerri was so in love with Monique that he would do anything for her. He also told me that Jerri's black CLK was in Monique's name. Wesley told me that Jerri used to pay the car note late all the time—I wonder how he knew that. He also told me that Monique never fucked Jerri. It was obvious that Monique painted a different picture to Wesley. The stories were crazy. Wesley went on and on. It was all news to me, but I didn't say a word to J; I kept it all inside.

I didn't believe most of the stories for a few reasons. I knew that Monique and Jerri had an intimate relationship. She was always buying things for Jerri, almost like a sugar momma. Monique used to call Jerri all the time. She called one night, around 1:30 AM, and I flipped out on him. I wasn't with the bullshit. He kicked that big brother–big sister game. Yeah, right. I wasn't falling for that okey doke, and we weren't going to sleep until I got some clarity on what was going on, so he finally confessed. He told me that he use to fuck her, and I died laughing.

"What are you laughing for?" he asked.

"What were you attracted to? I heard that girl look like she got Down syndrome," I said, still laughing.

"Ya'll, chicks is crazy," he said as he giggled.

"Why are *you* laughing?"

"She does look like ... She was fine back in the day. I always kept that image of her—and she got real pretty hair, too."

"So that's your excuse? You fucked her 'cause she was Quan's baby mom."

"Whatever, Neshela!"

"Well, you better tell her that Miami is here this weekend." I believed he fucked her cause she was the dude's baby mom—you know how that shit go; everybody want to fuck the head man's lady or ex-lady. That's the only excuse that I could come up with, 'cause her days were over—over!

Chapter 10

Miami Stay in Jersey

Jersey became my second home. Sometimes I would fly home and then fly back to Jersey the very next day; it was crazy. Angela would normally pick me up from the airport and drop me to an awaiting car on Jerri's block. We would usually have dinner at Ruth's Chris on Friday nights. Typically on Saturday morning, I'd go to the Spa at the Hilton in Short Hills while Jerri took care of business. By the time I returned to the house, there was generally a bag awaiting my arrival. It usually contained a jumpsuit and a pair of sneakers. Jerri though that I dressed too conservative, so he would buy me a jumpsuit and sneakers for each day that I was in Jersey. We'd normally go out on Saturday for dinner and a movie. Sundays we stayed in, playing video games and relaxing in the Jacuzzi. We had dinner early on Sundays because my flight generally departed at 7:00 PM. By now, I had accumulated clothes at Jerri's house, so I didn't have to pack anymore.

It wasn't until my ninth trip that I realized how special I was. Instead of Angela, Jerri picked me up from the airport this time. He was accompanied by a special guest, Mr. Jason, his son. I met his daughter, Charm, on several occasions, but I had never met Jason before. Jerri spoke of him often, but he had never brought him around. Later that evening, we took Jason to football practice in East Orange. Over dinner, Jerri explained how important his son was to him. He gave the details of the relationship that he had with Jason's mother, Adina. He made it clear that he wouldn't be with anyone that couldn't accept his relationship with Jason. I didn't understand at first, but he quickly clarified things. Jason isn't Jerri's biological son. I guess the average woman can't handle her man dealing with his ex and taking care of her child. However, it didn't bother me at all. I had a daughter, and I didn't have a problem accepting his son; I made that clear to him. Afterward, I received my very own set of house keys and an allowance. It was finally official.

Every once in a while, I would creep into town just because I missed him and, of course, to check on things. One time I lied and told Jerri that I would be in a meeting for most of day. I really boarded a flight to Newark, and when I landed in Jersey, I took a cab to East Orange Park. I knew that Jerri was at Jason's football practice. As I rode to the park, I sat on the phone with him, just to make sure that he didn't have a clue. I wanted to surprise him, and I did. I walked up behind and placed my hands over his eyes. "Guess who?"

He turned around, hugged me, and lifted me off the ground. "You crazy, Shela!"

"I know. I miss you, baby."

"Meeting, right! You crazy." He stood in disbelief. I had planned it so well.

I was scheduled to leave on Sunday as usual. However, Jerri asked if I could stay for the week. I made arrangements with my mother to keep Astar for the week and arranged to pick up a car from Quan so that I could have transportation while in Jersey. But I didn't inform Jerri of the arrangements that I made with Quan until he returned home. He asked me, "Why did you tell Quan that you were in town?"

"I didn't think it was a big deal!"

"Neshela, your Jersey friends won't be your friends for long if they know how often you come to town. Watch and see; they'll stop calling you soon."

I didn't understand at first, but in time I began to see how true some people were.

"Baby, just call City Express Limo services and set up an account," he said. "You should have Angela's number. Only use her to drive you around in the hood; never let her drive you to the house, okay? You don't need to get no car from Quan."

I didn't get it. Jerri talked to Quan occasionally, and, to my knowledge, they were cool, so I couldn't understand his statement. I didn't think he would be jealous of the friendship that Quan and I had. He knew that we're like family. But I followed his instructions anyway and opened an account with City Express Limo. Jerri wanted me to have two drivers; one for the hood and another to drive me around in the area that we lived. Ivan was to be my new driver while I was in Jersey.

The week would reveal all sorts of things. I was falling in love with a dope boy, and he made it easy. I was fully aware of what I was getting myself into. Jerri was the leader of a crime organization called the Firm. The Firm was responsible for distributing drugs across a small part of Newark. Alpine was the block that they represented and their meeting spot for all of their business deals.

What I didn't know that his baby mom was still in love with him. It was Friday evening, we were leaving Jason's football game, and Jerri decided to stop by his mother's house on Clinton Avenue. While Jason and I waited in car,

I noticed a green Acura driving slowly down the one-way street where we were parked. My instinct told me something was wrong. I checked the rearview mirror, only to see that Jerri was not paying any attention. I quickly jumped in the driver's seat, preparing for the worst. I pushed the brakes twice, hoping he would notice. He didn't. I told Jason to lay flat down on the floor as I put the car in gear; I was ready to pull off. Suddenly the Acura stopped, and so did my heart. There was no escape—the Acura was one hundred feet in front of me, I couldn't go anywhere. At that moment, a girl jumped out of the car.

I was so relieved; I died laughing inside. I called Liz to share the story, and we were crying laughing I was thinking some niggas was going to pull out heat. What I didn't notice was the kazoo going on behind me. Jason cried out, "Daddy!" I turned around, only to see tears rolling down his face.

"Baby, what's wrong?" I asked him.

Then I heard someone tapping on the window. "Open the door, bitch! Open the door!"

I quickly turned to my right, only to see the same chick that jumped out of the car, screaming, "Open the door! Open the door, bitch!" She looked so hurt. Then another woman appeared at the car. I assumed she was Jerri's mother. He looked just like her.

"Shitara, stop. She doesn't have anything to do with this. Come on, baby, stop acting like this," Jerri's mother said.

I know I had a puzzled look on my face—I was not sure as to what was going on. I just looked at her and continued to talk on the phone. "Yo Liz, this bitch is crazy."

"Neshela, what going on?" Liz asked.

"Shit, I don't know. This bitch is acting like an animal."

"Who is it?"

"I don't know!"

"Where J at?"

"I don't know," I answered.

"You going to get out?"

"Hell, No! I ain't fi'in fight no dumb bitch over no nigga—you know I'm too pretty for that bullshit."

As Jerri's mother continued to pull the bitch away, I noticed the large tattoo on the woman's back. It was a J with flowers and hearts around it. At that instant, she picked up a bottle and headed toward the car, and, out of nowhere, Jerri appeared. I couldn't make out his words—everyone was screaming. He picked the chick up by her neck and began to choke her. The bottle crashed into the sidewalk, and he threw her into the windshield. The entire car shook. I opened the door "Jerri, please. Let's go."

His family begged him to leave, but he continued to scream, "Bitch, we ain't together! You crazy. Get the fuck out of here! Stupid bitch." Blood was everywhere, and I called Mimi and Quan to pick me up. I have no tolerance for bullshit, and I felt that Jerri wasn't being honest. I just couldn't imagine that a woman would act that way if she had not been misled. I would have never expected Jerri to do that to anyone, a part of me felt sorry for her. I'm a woman first; I couldn't ignore her pain. However, it couldn't have ever been me; I couldn't live with the embarrassment. Not only was I, his new chick, there, but his family and her friends watched. It seemed that they couldn't pull him off her. She had to feel like the stupidest bitch in the world.

When we got home, I put Jason to bed and began to pack my clothes. Jerri pleaded with me to stay, "Neshela, I promise you I'm not with her. You see how often you're here. I gave you the key 'cause I want you to be here. I love the structure you put in my life. I love to come home every night to dinner and wake up to breakfast. Whatever it takes to prove it to you, please don't leave. I'll call my mother—she will tell you I'm not with that girl; she just my baby mom. Neshela, I haven't even fucked that girl since I started fucking with you. I swear."

I called Quan and told him that I was good; I decided to stay. He asked me if I was sure. I said, "Yes, I'm staying with my man." We giggled and hung up the phone.

The following day I was rewarded with a shopping spree at Short Hills Mall. We went to our regular spots: Gucci, Neiman Marcus, Fendi, and Dolce & Gabbana. We spent over six g's. Jerri walked out, holding his head. "Damn, you got me."

"No, baby. She got you. Better tell your bitch to stop acting like an animal. Then I'll stop acting like the queen of the jungle." For Shitara's five minutes of acting like an ass, I was rewarded! I wanted her to act like an ass again and again! And indeed she did.

The next few days would be a test of my patience, causing me to realize how unintelligent and young this little girl was. After the mall, Jerri made plans for us to have dinner at Ruth's Chris. He decided to invite Abdul and Husa. The plans were for everyone to meet up at 8:00 PM on Alpine. Jerri and I arrived around 8:15. He got out of the car to talk to Abdul. I was sitting in the car on the phone, as usual, talking to Liz, when Abdul jumped in the car and pulled off fast as hell.

"What the fuck is going on?" I screamed.

"Shela, I don't know"

"Where is J? Why the fuck are you driving like a maniac? I have a child to live for." Then I noticed the car following us. I immediately called Jerri's phone. He didn't give me a chance to say hello.

"Baby, I'm sorry," he said. "This bitch pulled up with her friends. I didn't want you to deal with the bullshit."

"This shit is crazy. Our dinner reservation is for 9:00. Jerri, I'm hungry."

"I don't know where this bitch at; I don't know what she got up her sleeves."

"Look, I don't care. She know where we lay our head at. Call your baby mom and tell her we'll be home around 11:00. I'm hungry, okay!"

"Let me speak to Abdul, Neshela." I gave Abdul the phone, and I heard Abdul say, "Man, don't worry. I ain't gonna let shit happen to her; we on our way back to the block."

I tried to grab the phone back as Abdul hung up. "Shit happen to who?" I asked. "Not me! Y'all must be crazy!" We returned to the block to pick up Jerri and Husa. I got out of the front seat to sit in the back with Jerri. He was apologizing, "Come here, baby, I'm sorry. Neshela, you heard her on the phone last night."

"Yeah, I know," I said. "Answer the phone; she going to keep calling."

He picked up his phone. "What Shitara? Why you keep calling my phone, you stupid ho? ... She doesn't want to speak to you!"

I looked at him. "Why she want to talk to me for? Tell her I said grow up."

She continued to call as we proceeded to Ruth's Chris. We arrived late for our reservation. As we walked in the door, we were greeted by the hostess, Sandy, "Hi, Mr. Hopkins. We missed you yesterday. I can seat you immediately, but not at your favorite table. Is that okay?"

"Sure, that will be fine. Thanks, baby."

"Tony will still be your server," Sandy said.

"That's great." Dinner was great as usual, but the night continued to go downhill. Unwanted guests showed up, ruining my night.

"Oh shit, is that what I think it is? Oh my God, let's go."

"It's just a roach, Neshela."

"Just a roach? I don't eat with roaches. Why are y'all looking at me crazy? That shit ain't funny; stop laughing. Where is the manager?"

After explaining to the manager about our visitor, Husa offered to show her the roach that he took of the wall next to us. She declined and thanked us for not overreacting and for keeping the matter quiet. She also offered to take care of our check, and of course we accepted. We decided to order desert and a few additional entrées; you know we had to be niggas. The check was only $732.00. We came out on top. I stayed in Jersey for another week to make my presence known and to make it understood that I wasn't going anywhere.

On Friday, we were back at our favorite spot. We spent the weekend in Atlantic City gambling, but Jerri got carry away this time—twenty thousand g's in two minutes—it was a record. I didn't understand it at all. *Gambling must be his outlet for something*, I thought. I just hadn't figured it out yet. We had been to Atlantic City on several occasions; I had witnessed Jerri gambling away thousands and thousands of dollars but never this fast. He wasn't even sick about it. I would have been dying. In fact, I was dying—and it wasn't even my money. "Damn, baby," I chided. "You can't keep doing this—twenty thousand today; what will it be tomorrow?"

"Neshela, give me a break. Please don't preach, not tonight, baby."

"I won't. I love you baby." It was obvious to me that Jerri had a serious gambling problem, but he seemed so happy. He made it so hard to talk about it, but the issue need to be addressed, so the following morning at breakfast I decided to bring it up. It was time for me to understand the

man that I was falling in love with. After an hour of a serious heart-to-heart, I respected and understood why he
chose to gamble. I didn't like it at all, but I understood. We
had some of the best times in Atlantic City for a couple
reasons: he was able to do whatever he wanted with his
money, without thinking of anyone's needs, and his cell
phone never worked well at the Taj.

Chapter 11

Separating from the Crew

Jerri had witnessed countless conversations with my acquaintances. I used to talk to them every day, and he noticed that I received fewer calls. Indeed, my time with the crew had come to an end. Separating from the crew was difficult. It wasn't like a complete divorce; we still talked on a regular basis. I even stopped by Mimi's shop when I was in town, and Hakim or Summer would press my hair occasionally. We were still cool—we just didn't talk the same. Our conversations didn't last forever anymore; they were quick and to the point. We were all so caught up in our own lives; everyone was so distant. Jerri had warned me of this day, but there is no preparing for this.

What I didn't know about my Jersey friends was that their pack ran small. Their circles were all connected, and one chick, Monique, kept them all informed of each other's business. When I heard about that, I understood why Wesley talked so much. It became clear why I was his friend. It was simple; I was an outlet for the Jersey crew to express their real feelings about everything. Technically, I didn't know anyone, so who was I going to tell? I was from Miami; I didn't live in New Jersey. Their secrets were safe with me. But things had changed; I was always in Jersey and I was dating Jerri.

As I lay in silence, reminiscing on the old days, how much I missed Quan and Mimi, Jerri asked me, "How did you meet them, Neshela?"

"Who?" I asked.

"Quan!"

"Oh, the crew." I am sure that he already knew, but I guess this was a test of truth and trust. I told him the story of leaving Club Bed on South Beach, and how Wesley tapped on my window; it was four years ago. "Why do you ask?"

"I'm just curious, baby," he said. I was fully aware that Jerri and Wesley were enemies, but I continued to act like I had no clue.

"So, you know Wesley?" he asked.

"Yes, I just told you that, Jerri! Why? You know Wesley?"

"Naw."

"What's that supposed to mean? I can tell when you're lying, Jerri." Jerri was fully aware of the whole story; he knew how I met the crew and I know he knew. He and Mack were close; in fact they spoke on a daily basis. Did he really think that I was going to lie? When Jerri saw me in Club Deco a couple years earlier, he asked some people about me, and they informed him that I was from Miami. He even asked my friends if they were sure that I wasn't the Feds—this nigga was on top of his game. Jerri checked shit out before he jumped into it. And there he was, trying to play on my intelligence; he must have thought I was a dumb bitch.

Ironically, that morning my phone rang and it's Wesley. Unfortunately for me, my cell phone was sitting right next to Jerri. He handed me the phone, instructing me to answer it, and I did. Wesley and I talked for a minute. I was pleased that Jerri could see how we conversed and that we were really just friends. He never questioned me about Wesley, but I was sure that his thoughts were clouded, wondering about the type of relationship that Wesley and I had. I continued chatting with Wesley for a few weeks. However, I only talked to him when I was with Jerri. I would intentionally put the volume on my phone up, just so that Jerri could hear us. Even if he acted like he wasn't listening. I wanted him to be secure about the whole thing. Little did I know how much this stunt would pay off later.

That evening, we went shopping at Neiman Marcus, Jerri's favorite place. Shopping was his thing, and I loved doing it with him. Jerri often treated me like a baby doll, picking and choosing things for me to try on. We'd be in Neiman Marcus forever, and I enjoyed every moment of it just as much as he enjoyed watching me change and the attention we got from everyone around us. I felt like Julia Roberts in *Pretty Woman*. After our shopping spree, we had dinner with Abdul at Delta's in New Brunswick. Delta's is a new-age soul-food restaurant with a relaxing ambience and good old-fashioned Southern hospitality. The macaroni and cheese there is to die for.

The following day we were supposed to go on a plane ride to tour the city but we woke up late, so we spent most of the day daydreaming. We drove around in Fairfield, Verona, and Caldwell, looking at houses—real houses, mansions! These mansions were beautiful; they ranged between seven and eight million dollars. One of the best things about our relationship was that we could dream. We were from different worlds, but when we're together we shared the same dream, a life of luxury.

When we returned home, we decided to spend the rest of the day reading, and with Jerri reading, we could finish a book in a day. *Caught 'em Slippin'* by Al-Saadiq Banks was our choice for the evening. We cuddled in bed and escaped in the characters of Miranda and Sha-Rock. Jerri finished the book in just four and half hours; we spent the rest of the day lying in bed, reminiscing on how everything happened so fast. We're caught up! We met one month, talked for two months, fucked on the fourth month, and I was falling dangerously in love. He always did something to keep me on my feet. One day, Jerri replayed one of our conversations from a few weeks earlier. It blew my mind. He had recorded our conversation; in fact, he recorded several of our conversations, and when I asked him why, he said, "So that when you're not here, I could always hear your voice. You know you're my better half, Shela. I really love you."

I'm crying inside; I knew that he adored me, but I didn't realize that he really loved me. I never thought that I could fall in love with Jerri, the arrogant dude from Mimi's salon. I don't know how it happened or when; I just know it happened. The simple "I love you" has so much meaning; we shared passion. I loved the shit out of him. No one treated me that way he did, and there was nothing that I could have wanted for.

It was time for me to make another surprise trip to Jersey, and this time it was easy. It's Abdul's birthday, and Jerri already informed me that he would be out late. Some people from Abdul's school were throwing Abdul a birthday party, and Jerri planned to attend. *Perfect!* I took a late flight into Jersey. Ivan picked me up; I told him not to say a word to Jerri. When I got to the house, it was around 12:20 AM. I brushed my teeth and jumped in the bed. I'm sound asleep when Jerri arrived home at 2:30 AM. I didn't even hear him come up the stairs. I woke up to his soft whisper,

"Baby, I almost killed you. Why do you have the covers over your head?"

"What?" I opened my eyes, and Jerri was holding his gun a few inches away from my head. "Oh my God," I screamed.

"Shela," he said. He still looked confused. "I don't know what the fuck is going on."

"Jerri, get that gun away from my face!"

"Shela" he exhaled, and as he whispered my name, I saw the worry on his face.

"Baby, I didn't mean to worry you. I just wanted to surprise you; I'm sorry, baby."

"Shela, don't do that shit." I got up to help him take his clothes off. I could tell that he had a little too much to drink. I think he realized he almost lost me, out of his life completely. That made him hold me extremely tight throughout the night while we slept.

Chapter 12

Meeting His Mom

Our relationship continued to grow. My weekend visits turned into weeks, which turned into months. We began to act like a family. We both changed our cell phone numbers. I required that Jerri be home every night at 7:00 PM for dinner. I also accompanied him to Jason's football practice four days a week. Our most intimate time was on Wednesdays. Jerri read to me on Wednesdays; he was a great reader. Our favorite authors were Al-Saadiq Banks and Terri Woods. I also required that Jerri fuck me every morning. It was my way of being an ass. Shitara, Charm's mom, wrecked her car; therefore, Jerri had to drop Charm to the nursery—or should I say to his auntie's house—every morning. He thought I didn't know that he always took Shitara to work too, so I fucked him every morning faithfully, giving him just enough time to make it out the door, leaving no time to shower or wash off. He would wear that same red jumpsuit every morning.

It's only one thing that I hated about our relationship—drama. We didn't have much of it, but when we did, we did. It's usually at the hands of Shitara; from her child-support stunts. She claimed that Jerri wasn't doing his part, and She threatened to go through the State for more child support. There was always something with her. Charm had weekly hospital visits for fevers whenever I was in town, but the best stunt was "Charm's out milk or food." This one usually took place around 9:00 PM. When she knew I was in town, she wouldn't allow Jerri to bring Charm to the house. Childish shit. If she only knew every time her daughter spent a night, she slept right next to me. I am not into the bullshit. I treated her child like she was mine, just as I did with Jason. I guess she didn't realize that I was not going anywhere.

We'd been together for a while when Jerri finally decided to invite his mother over for dinner. I was appalled at the timing. Earlier that day, we attended Jason's last football game of the season. This lady sat less than ten feet away from me and didn't say a mumbling word. When I attempted to speak to her, she acted like she didn't hear me. When we made eye contact, she rolled her eyes at me. I didn't tell him of her childish act until he told me she was coming over for dinner. Did he really think I was going to cook dinner for her?

"Neshela, you're being emotional," he said.

"J, don't play with me."

"That just how she is, baby. She didn't mean anything. But if you don't want to cook dinner, you don't have to. I'll never make you uncomfortable in this house. I want you to cook dinner. I told her all about them stuffed potatoes that you be making. I'll call and tell her you're not gon' cook anymore."

"Okay, I'll cook, J."

"You're calling me J today! Just make sure you make them stuffed potatoes."

The hours flew by. It's already 7:00 PM when Jerri arrived home with his mother, brother, and sister. It is seven of us; Jason and Astar was at the house too. I served stuffed potatoes, steak, and broccoli. It was definitely a memorable night. I hadn't been feeling good all day; I had stomach cramps. But I was so excited that Jerri's mother was coming over. Even with the slick shit from earlier, I was still excited. It's his mother. She and I greeted each other at the stove. Her first comment was, "Can you cook?"

"Of course I can cook. That why your son come home every night." Within about five minutes, I began to place the plates on the table. I walked back to the stove to make Jerri's and my plate when his mother made a smart comment. "I guess I'm supposed to eat with my hand like an animal."

"Mom, you tripping," Jerri said. "We don't have no maid around here; I'll get you a fork."

I was standing at the stove, furious. I forgot the silverware. But if I had set the table properly, would she have known the salad fork from the dinner fork? I was a second away from walking straight out of the kitchen. *Fuck this dinner shit. My stomach is killing me and I am not up for more slick shit.* Out of respect, I didn't—or couldn't—say anything slick back. I think this bothered me more. Jerri stood beside me and whispered in my ear. "Baby, you need help," he said as he kissed my cheek. I rolled my eyes, and he giggled, knowing she just crawled under my skin. And to make matters worse, when she walked out the door she called my daughter "nappyhead"!

Ball-headed bitch! I can't get the words out of my mouth fast enough, and Jerri would kill me, so I didn't bother to say anything. God knows I wanted to.

The next morning, we had a busy day ahead of us. We planned to hang out with the kids for the entire weekend. Jerri and I usually attended most of the Giants games, but this Saturday, the kids joined us. It's Jerri's and Astar's birthday weekend—their birthdays are a day apart. After the game we had cake and ice cream to celebrate. I enjoyed family events, I just loved it when the four of us went out.

Jason and Astar were so funny together. I tried to have family night as often as possible. I hated that Charm couldn't join us, but her mother wouldn't allow it.

The following evening, we went to dinner at Mr. Chow. We were accompanied by Malik and his girl. When I enter Malik's van, Melissa, this red chick from Miami, was sitting in the front seat. I stared at her, thinking, *I know her face, I even know her name, but can't remember where from.* I sat in that backseat trying to figure it out. Jerri knew it was puzzling me. I hate not knowing, so I finally asked him, "Baby, where do I know her from?"

He doesn't respond. He just giggles, assuring me that I know her. As we drove to Manhattan, I sat there, confused. Finally I decided to just ask her. "Where do I know you from?"

"Miami," this smart-mouthed bitch said.

"I know that, but do I know you?"

"You're little one, sister. I use to fuck with your brother."

"Oh, shit," I said. This was Melissa, Malik's chick that lived in Atlanta. My brother use to have a place with her. When my brother got indicted, my mother had to pick up his BMW from Melissa. *Damn, it a small world!*

We sat at the table making small talk while Malik ordered for everyone. We had been to Mr. Chow several times, but Malik was a true regular. We spent two hours eating and conversing about Miami and New Jersey.

The total for dinner at Mr. Chow was only $1,158. Jerri pulled out six hundred in singles. I could have crawled under the table. Jerri would send me to the market with two or three hundred in singles, but not at Mr. Chow! How ghetto was this! It had to be the most embarrassing shit ever, and no one seemed to care but me. Melissa pulled another bundle of singles from her blue and white Dolce and Gabbana bag to cover the remanding balance of the bill. Our server was just as shocked as I was; he walked away, speaking another language. I could feel the eyes of the other servers watching us, but before the waiter could get far, Jerri called him back and exchanged the singles with hundreds. I turned to Jerri and thanked him for saving me the embarrassment.

Chapter 13

Decisions

When we first started talking, I was kind of skeptical. I knew he was wrong for me. I never liked street dudes, but it was our conversations that kept me attached. We're closer than I realized—so close that he was growing inside of me. I always wanted more children, but after the ectopic pregnancy with Christopher, back in 2000, I was told that I wouldn't able to have any more children without medical assistance. For that reason, after our AIDS/HIV test results came back negative, we began to have unprotected sex. The next month I was pregnant, right along with everyone else: Mimi; Jennifer, Wesley's girlfriend; Doman's girlfriend, Robin. It's something in Jersey's water that September; everybody was pregnant.

Jerri and I took the pregnancy test together after dinner on Wednesday evening. I was not sure if I was ready for the responsibility. I been sick as a dog, my stomach churning. I was always nauseous; I had the worst morning sickness. Every morning, I'd wake up at 3:00 AM because of my stomach turning. When I was pregnant with Astar, I didn't recall ever being sick. Therefore, this was all new to me. Jerri determined that I was pregnant with his son. He said only his son would kick my ass like that. Moon was killing me—I decided that my first son's name would be Moon. Jerri hated it at first, but it grew on him.

I was so grateful to be pregnant from Jerri. He was very supportive. He took good care of me, even when I went to Miami. He'd call Liz to make sure that she checked on me for the few days that I was in town. In Jersey, when I woke up every morning at 3:00 AM, Jerri would hold me close and rub my stomach until the cramps went away. He would play "Still Got It" by Jamie Foxx and Common. That song always makes me smile.

It's our first ultrasound appointment with the doctor's office in Mt. Clair; I was so excited. We arrived at the doctor's office just in time for our appointment. The nurse quickly went over a few documents while she took my blood using a thin butterfly needle. Within minutes, I was laying flat on my back while the radiologist rubbed warm gel on my stomach to begin the ultrasound. I don't know why, but when the doctor gave us the due date, June 12, 2006, Jerri lit up. He even asked the doctor if he was sure of the baby's due date. The date was special to Jerri—I was not sure why—All I knew was he seemed happy about the whole thing.

That evening we had dinner with Jerri's cousin, Mike, and his wife. We decided to have dinner at Jezebel in Manhattan. It's a hell of a car ride. Mike's wife had a mouth on her. I was feeling her at first, but she got a little carried away. Jerri and I sat quietly in the backseat as their bickering went on and on. She wouldn't shut up for shit. It's a straight power struggle between the two of them. This had to be the worst double date ever. Don't get me wrong, she was really nice and friendly; it just seemed like they were having some personal issues and maybe they should have stayed in. After riding in circles for twenty minutes, we finally arrived just in time for our reservation. It was a long night with the two of them, but we made the best of it. Their relationship was one that Jerri admired. He always told stories about them and how they had been through so much together. I still can't understand what it is about their relationship that Jerri loves. Shit, to me, they needed a divorce and Mike needed a backbone; their relationship could use one or the other. I fell asleep on the car ride home. I refused to listen to them.

After the first six weeks, things got better. I still woke up at 3:00 AM, but my stomach didn't churn as much. Jerri took on the house duties. He dropped the laundry to the Wash & Fold and cleaned the house for me; he even went to the grocery store for me. I had to remind him that I was only two months, and I was still able to do my womanly duties. I didn't even cook that often anymore; we ate out most of the time at Toscani, a little Italian restaurant on Belmont Avenue.

On Thursdays, Jerri brought home greens from the African restaurant. They had a unique taste that I enjoyed, but this Thursday, Jerri didn't come home with greens. Instead, he wore a bloodstained shirt. I knew something was wrong when I heard Jerri running up the stairs. I never dreamed of this day. Jerri quickly told me the story of what had just went down while loading his .45 and running back out of the house.

"Baby, I love you!" I yelled after him.

"I'll be right *back*, don't worry!" These were the last words that flew from his mouth as the door closed. The crazy part about the whole thing was that I was not worried at all. I lay on the couch as if nothing was going on. Shortly after, I went in the kitchen, where I began to prepare dinner; I knew he was coming home. And indeed he did.

The drama between the Firm and another crew got crazy. Every other day, it's something, and the gun battles were taking lives. Four people were killed that week. Malik's van was shot up—it was a total of thirty-two bullets. *Thank*

God Malik wasn't in the van at the time of the shooting. I could barely sleep at night. The cameras at our house had an automatic device that detected sound for a two-mile radius. We could hear all types of conversations and it kept me up at night. This new pressing beef made me analyze my whole situation and the reality of being pregnant. I was pregnant from a dope boy, and the one thing that dope boys don't offer is security. I realized that I enjoyed the benefits of the relationship, but I knew that I was not woman enough to have another child from a man with no future. No matter how much I loved him or how much of a blessing our baby was because I was told I couldn't have children. I am selfish and I loved myself more.

As I lay in the bed with Jerri, I told him that I didn't think our relationship was ready for a guest and that I wanted to have an abortion. He simply asked me if I was crazy and ended the conversation. Jerri acted as if he didn't hear me and never mentioned it again. Jerri wasn't into abortions; he had lost a son a couple years earlier, a stillborn.

I felt trapped and I knew I couldn't have this baby, but I needed support for the action I was planning to take. See, street niggas don't die of old age; they usually die one of three ways: 1) They get shot and killed. 2) They die in prison. 3) They die of AIDS. So I called Mimi first, Liz second, and Quan third. Only one of them supported me and understood my concern. My mother didn't even support me on this one. I think everyone was caught up in the fact that I couldn't have children and how much I loved him.

The next few weeks in our house were different. I was depressed and miserable, and Jerri just ignored it. He knew exactly what is wrong with me—I didn't want our baby. I flew home to Miami, where I planned to have my abortion without his approval. But my soul wouldn't let me. I had no idea what was going on with my body. It's around 7:00 PM when I felt like I was dying. I only had enough physical power to dial 911. When the paramedics arrived, they rushed me to Memorial Regional Hospital. It's at the moment when I hear my son's heartbeat that I realized that I wanted him. I wanted my baby.

The tears rolled down my face as I began to go back and forth, trying to reason with myself, *Why should I keep this child?* Considering I was a high-risk pregnancy, I was held overnight for observation. When the doctor entered my room, he informed me that I had lost a lot of blood; however, things were going to be fine. He just needed to run a few more tests. I was released from the hospital the following day. Jerri insisted that I fly back to Jersey, and I did. After seeing how much stress my body was going through, Jerri finally decided to talk about it, and we agreed to the abortion. On one condition, he said, still trying to change my mind: he would never speak to me again.

I had to do it. I made the appointment with Dr. Skit, a private doctor in Union, New Jersey. I had never had an abortion before, and I was not about to go to no one's clinic. When the day had finally come; the appointment was for 2:00 PM. We had missed three prior appointments; we were dealing with my emotional imbalance. It had to be hard on Jerri. As we sat in the lobby together, waiting for the nurse to call me to the back, my mother and Mimi called, both asking me if I was sure that I was doing the right thing. I had to do what I had to do. The nurse opened the door and my name was called.

"Jerri, I am sorry," I said as I got up.

"Baby, I understand. I love you. We'll do it again, don't worry," he said. And with those words, I wiped the tears from his eyes and proceeded to the door. I knew at that point that we would still be together, even though he'd threatened to never speak to me again. He couldn't stay away for long.

I'll never forget that day. No one told me it would be that way. I woke up during the middle of the procedure. I heard everything. I was numb, but I heard everything—the metal clicking, the eerie noises. I heard it all and I promised to God and Jerri that I would never do it again. After it was over, we went home, where I curled up in bed and cried myself to sleep. I was scheduled to leave Newark at 9:50 PM, but Mimi talked Jerri into letting me stay. Jerri continued to be supportive at first, but it's obvious that things were different. Jerri would periodically say rude things like, "I can't believe you killed my son." He would say cruel things just to piss me off.

I only stayed in Jersey for a week and half after the abortion. I decided it's time to go home, we needed some time apart. I believed this was what he wanted; he just didn't know how to say it. The first few days, we didn't talk much. He couldn't get over the abortion; it put a strain on our relationship. For some reason, he thought I felt that I was too good to have his child. That wasn't the case; I just wanted more. Jerri limited himself to just hustling, and I wanted more. Every time I spoke of new things, like staring a business or opening a nursery, he would just brush it off. He was content with hustling.

I'd lived that life; my mother pushed weight for my uncles. My people didn't petty hustle; they did big shit. My mother flew kilos of drugs from the Bahamas on her boyfriend's private jet. I've sat in on a trial of my mother's friends and watched them get years on top of years. My mother's best friend, Sharon, got twenty-five years when she got caught. I lost two uncles to the streets; my brother got shot in the head because of the streets. I didn't want any part of the street; *fuck* the street. I hated the streets and I was determined not have any part of the streets in my life. I had no plan to fall in love with a street nigga; it just happened. And I couldn't convince him that at the end of the day the streets don't give a fuck about him. It was only the product that he sold. He was just as much of a victim as the families that the drugs destroy.

Chapter 14

The Aftermath

I truly regretted the abortion, and I was willing to do anything to make things right again. Jerri and I used to be so happy, now we were just regular. I guess he was doing him, so I decided to do me. I flew home on Sunday; Liz knew that I was feeling down, so she planned a girl's night out. South Beach was our destination. We met a few dudes and ended up having dinner with some corny-ass Miami niggas. I hated Miami niggas; it was just something about them that turned me completely off. Liz suggested that I talk to a dude, considering he offered to take us to dinner. She thought that it would help me get Jerri off my mind. "Since you're back in Miami for good, girl, you need somebody to pass time with," she said. She's right, so I exchanged numbers with the dude, Allen, and we began to communicate on a daily basis.

To my surprise, Jerri flew to Miami the following weekend so that we could spend some time together. I booked a reservation at Trump Plaza on Bal Harbor Island. I wanted to be close to the mall, and Bal Harbor is one of the best high-end malls in Miami. Shopping and partying was the only thing on the agenda for the weekend. Our relationship needed a bounce back. Jerri's flight landed late on Friday night. We had dinner at Mango's Tropical Café, conveniently located in the center of South Beach. It was one of Jerri's favorite restaurants. Mango's is world-renowned for its exciting entertainment and tropical ambience. Jerri just had to visit whenever he was in Miami.

We spent most of the day shopping on Saturday; we had dinner at Houston's that evening. We went in early because we had to wake up in the early hours for church on Sunday morning. I always went to church when I was in Miami. After church, we had brunch at Don Shula. We spent the evening walking the beach. Jerri, Liz, and I planned to party the night away. We went to Club Opium on South Beach and had two bottles of Patron. They were fucked up and so was I, but I didn't drink, so it wasn't the liquor that had me. Then, I couldn't help but notice this dude across the room. He kept looking in our direction, but I couldn't make out his face. I decided to pull the famous bathroom trick, and off I went. I walked right in to Christopher Brian Mathis. *Oh, shit!* I was so ready to go. Of all the people in the world, I would have never thought that I would see Christopher at Opium.

After a two-week separation, Jerri asked me to come back home. I was back in Jersey right in time for the holidays. We decided to cook Thanksgiving dinner at our house. Jerri invited his mother and father over; his mother brought cabbage and corned beef. We had a traditional Thanksgiving, and we all enjoyed dinner that evening. Charm got most of the attention; she ran around the house in her walker, playing with everyone. It was a wonderful evening, but of course a smart-ass comment had to come out of Mrs. Hopkins's mouth. "You know, my children don't eat cornbread, and your stuffing taste just like cornbread," she said.

But it was a good day, and I was not about to let her ruin my mood. I said, "I didn't know they didn't eat cornbread; I do make my stuffing with Jiffy mix. I don't think they noticed it, because most of them are finished eating. Besides,

Jerri eats cornbread all the time around here—maybe you don't make it as good as I do! But, you know, you have to give me the recipe for your corned beef and cabbage, it's really good. Too salty, but good; it is real good and salty!"

That night when Jerri joined me in bed, I asked, "Jerri, why doesn't your mother like me? What's her issue with me?"

"I don't think it's that she doesn't like you. She's just like that, Neshela."

"Is it because she's close with Shitara?"

"I don't know, baby."

"Well, she doesn't have to give me attitude when she here. I didn't break up your happy home, Jerri, and I'm not really into the mother-in-law thing; I got a mother. She doesn't have to like me."

"Who said she don't like you? That how my mother is, Neshela. I'm sure she doesn't mean anything. Stop letting that shit get to you, baby. Let's talk about you moving up here."

"Relocating permanently!"

"Yes, instead of going back and forth."

"I have to find a job first," I said. "And it's too boring to live up here all the time. Besides, I don't have any friends, and plus it is too dirty here. I don't want to live here."

"Oh, now you too good to live in Jersey?"

"Don't act like that; you know I hate this dirty-ass city. If it wasn't for you, I wouldn't be here."

"You don't need a job, Neshela."

"Ok, Jerri I'll just sit in the house."

But I began to look for a position in New Jersey or New York. I decided that I would make New Jersey my new permanent address. I planned to move up in February of the next year. It was just a few months away. The following week, I landed a few job interviews. The most promising position was an executive assistant position at World Yacht-ing, the largest yachting marine company in the world. The interview was in New York. I thought it went well.

That weekend Jerri invited his family to join us for din-ner, and we went out to Ekkio in Livingston, New Jersey. I guess Jerri thought if we had dinner at a restaurant, he wouldn't have to worry about his mother finding some-thing to complain about. It really didn't matter anymore for me, I didn't care if she liked me or not. I just sat at the table in la-la land. I only spoke when I'm spoken to. My mind was elsewhere. I was too busy thinking of other things. I seen Mimi earlier today; she's so cute and pregnant. She made me want to be pregnant again. After dinner, we dropped Jason home first, and then Jerri's family. We made three stops because Jerri's brother and his two kids joined us for dinner. I couldn't wait to get home; I wanted to be pregnant and I needed to tell Jerri.

When we arrived at the house I told him I wanted to be pregnant. He looked pissed. "Neshela, I'm *not* going through that shit with you again. You were just pregnant a month ago. In fact, you was three months pregnant. Re-member, you had an abortion; you wasn't ready to have a baby from a dope boy, *right*? Remember, those were your words."

"I didn't say it like that, Jerri. I'm serious, I want to be pregnant. I want to have our baby."

"Oh, really. I guess you had an epiphany."

"Fuck you, Jerri. You don't even know what the word means. Forget about it, and forget I even said anything," I said as I started to leave the room.

"Neshela, come here."

"Don't worry about it, Jerri. Bath or shower? I'm going to run the water."

"Let's take a bath so we can talk."

"Jerri, that's okay!"

"No really, let's talk about it," he said.

We spent an hour in the tub talking about our relationship. I was so excited; Jerri and I agreed to try again. I flew home the following day to meet with my doctor so we could discuss my options. Dr. Newman gave me many different opinions but stated that IVF would be the best and most successful process. IVF is a technique in which a woman's egg cells are fertilized by sperm outside the woman's womb. The fertilized egg is then transferred to the patient's uterus with the intent to establish a successful pregnancy. It is costly—very costly—but we decided to move forward with it.

Jerri and Jason flew to Miami a week after I met with Dr. Newman. Jerri delivered one of my many Christmas gifts: we went to the doctor to begin the process for the IVF. I also received a Michelle watch. It's nice but I was expecting a Rolex. I had talked about the Rolex for a few months; that usually all it took for me to get what I want. Jerri quickly informed me that it wasn't going down like that. Especially after he had just spent sixty-three hundred on in vitro fertilization. I was grateful for the little twenty-eight-hundred-dollar watch. I was ever more grateful for the in vitro fertilization—this gift was priceless. My gift to Jerri was a skiing trip to Denver, Colorado, for New Year's.

Jerri and I took the kids to Disney World as an early Christmas gift. We spent the weekend there. It was an early Christmas, and it was wonderful. I had been to Disney World over eighty times, and Astar, my eight-year-old daughter, had been at least thirteen times, but Jerri and Jason had never been. This made the trip more memorable.

When we returned to Miami from Orlando, we dropped

the kids to my mother. We decided to hang out on South
Beach. We had dinner at Jerri's favorite Miami restaurant,
Mango's. The food was delicious, but I'm sure it was his
favorite because the women walk around half naked. Mango's meant "entertainment." Live music and continuous
choreographed dance shows will provide a memorable
evening. You can never forget dinner at Mango's Tropical
Café. As I sat across the table from Jerri, I thought of the
first time we had dinner together at Spain in New Jersey. I
didn't even like him then; now I'm so in love with this man.
After the abortion we became distant, but things were getting better. He was the perfect man, and there was so many
reasons that I stayed with him—regardless of how much I
didn't want a street nigga. He was truly one in a million. I
adored the things that he'd do for me and the way that he
loved me. After going back and forth to the doctor, they
finally confirmed that I was pregnant. I was extremely
happy. Our due date was September 3, 2006. We had something to look forward to.

I flew to Jersey to deliver the news. I had to tell him in
person. *We did it again!* We spent most of the weekend in
the house cuddling. It was cold in Jersey, and I hate being
cold. The bed was my favorite place when the temperature
was below 40 degrees. Jerri walked in the house and told
me to get dressed for the game. I wanted to get lost under
the sheets. "It's 30 degrees outside! Do we have to go?" I
asked.

"No! We don't have to; it just the 76ers," he answered.
I quickly jumped out of the bed. I loved Allen Iverson. I
wouldn't miss his game if it was thirty below. "You better
hurry," Jerri said, "we're going to be late."

"Don't worry, I'll be ready in five minutes," I assured
him. We made it to the game at the end of the first quar-
ter—we had to pick up Alba, one of Jerri's little mans (he

ran one of Jerri's safe houses). When we finally arrived, we rushed in the arena. I was freezing my ass off.

It's time to say goodbye. I had been in Jersey for over a week and it's time for me to go back to Miami. I had a few things to take care of. Besides, I only planned to be in Jersey for a day, to share the news with Jerri. I missed my flight seven times in the past week, mostly because I didn't want to leave, but I couldn't miss this flight. I had a doctor's appointment the next day that I couldn't miss. While in route to the airport, Jerri decided to make a few stops, and, unknown to us, two local kids decided to pick this day to play behind the wheel. They backed right into us, going at least 30 miles an hour. The car smacked the right side of the rental car that we're driving. The little boy jumps out of the car and began hauling ass. Jerri chased him around the block and dragged him back to the scene. The second little boy didn't even attempt to run. At this point, everyone was standing outside of John's Place, watching the scene. To make matters worse, the rental car that we're driving was in Raven's name. Raven and Jerri was as close as brother and sister, but they weren't really related by blood. By the time the police arrived, Jerri vanished, and Raven was on the scene as if she been driving the car the whole time. No one even realized what just happened. Raven was a hell of an actress—she had me thinking we were there from the beginning. When the little boys attempted to tell the police there was a man driving the car, they just brushed it under the mat. Considering several witnesses saw the little boy running from the scene, they only saw the man as a good person that chased the boy down. No one saw who was driving the car in the first place—it's just Raven and me.

I had to reschedule my doctor's appointment and put everything on hold. Jerri was going through an emotional crisis—someone had stolen one of his safes from his grandmother's house. He was a wreck. We didn't discuss how much money was in the safe. I didn't want to know. My job was just to comfort him and keep him calm about the whole thing. Only three people knew where the safe was, and no one had broken into the house. Therefore, if he kept his mind clear, he could easily figure it out. I had my own person in mind, but I chose not to share. I just supported him during these times.

The following weekend, we attended one of Jerri's family functions. It's his little cousin's birthday party. We pulled up to the Chinese Buffet at the same time as Mike and his wife. We entered the small restaurant and headed straight to the back to greet the birthday girl. She is such a pretty little girl; it's her fifth birthday and she's celebrating. I sat at the table next to one of Jerri's older cousins, Tiffany. We made small talk—she was currently enrolled in college and her major was the same as mine, psychology. So we chitchatted until Jerri interrupted us to drag me over to the head table where his mother's sisters sat. God knows, if they're anything like her, I didn't want to meet them, but he gave me no option.

"Auntie, this is Neshela, my wife." When we found out I was pregnant with Moon, Jerri started calling me his wife whenever we met people—I wasn't just going to be his baby mom.

"Your wife!" she said. "Wasn't you just married to that other girl?"

"Auntie—" he started.

"I joking baby," she said. Then she turned to me. "How are you?"

"I'm fine, thank you ma'am," I answered sweetly.

"Ma'am! I'm not that old! Just call me Auntie. You're a beautiful girl. I heard a lot about you. You better take care of my nephew, and don't go havin' no baby too soon." I laughed. If only she'd known I was already pregnant from Jerri for the second time.

I finally made it home a week later. I planned to stay for a few weeks; I needed to spend some time with my daughter.

Chapter 15

Rude Awakening

I took the red-eye into New Jersey on Friday night. Ivan was off, so Jerri had to pick me up from the airport. I was so happy to be home, right until 7:03 AM. Jerri's cell phone began to vibrate. It was 7:21 and the phone was still lighting up like a Christmas tree.

"Jerri, just answers the fucking phone. She gon' keep calling, and you know it."

"She doesn't want shit," he said.

"*Answer* it."

He picked up the phone, looking pissed. "*What*, Shitara? … I got shit to do. I can't; call my mother …I'll call you back."

After he hung up, I asked, "Jerri, what wrong? Charm got a fever?"

"No, Neshela. She say she needs to get her hair done!"

"What?"

"Shitara need to get her hair done," he said again.

"What wrong with that, Jerri? Go get Charm. We ain't got shit to do today. Beside, the girl needs a fucking break. I'll start cooking breakfast. Go get her."

"You sure? I think Shitara trying to be funny."

"It seven o'clock in morning, Jerri. She not joking. Maybe she got a date tonight. Tell her I said hey."

"Stop trying to be funny, Neshela."

"On your way back, stop by Shop Rite and bring some orange juice and bacon. Love you."

Jerri got dressed to go in pick up Charm. A few minutes later, I turned the shower on and began to brush my teeth. As I looked out of the window, I noticed a gold car parked across the street. I couldn't ID the person sitting in the car, so I went to the camera monitor to get a clearer view. I still couldn't recognize the person or the car. I immediately called Jerri to tell him of the visitor, but he didn't answer the phone, and by then the car was gone. The car sat in front of the house for exactly twenty-two minutes. I was puzzled, but I went ahead and took a shower.

After I got out of the shower, Jerri called. "I'm on my way home. What did you need from the store?"

"Orange juice and bacon. By the time you get here, it'll be time for lunch."

"Really I'm outside, smart-ass. I just wanted to make sure I have everything. Put on clothes. Emmet is going to eat breakfast with us; we coming up right now."

I ran in the bathroom to slip on a pair of slacks and shirt. The gold car was back. *Who the hell is that?* The front door opened. I shouted, "Jerri, come here, hurry!"

"What wrong?"

"Just hurry!" I didn't want to take my eyes off the car this time. Jerri walked in the bathroom holding Charm.

"What happen, Shela?" he asked.

"That gold car was here earlier, and it left. Now it's back. There was a dude sitting in it. Earlier, he sits out there for like twenty minutes."

"Baby, that Emmet car."

"Why the fuck was he sitting out there? He scared the hell out of me."

"You crazy, girl. What up with breakfast?"

"Okay, calm down. Let me play with Charm for a minute. Then I'll cook." Charm was the cutest dark-skinned little girl; she was always so happy, always smiling. Playing with Charm always calmed me down. I loved playing with her. When I finished playing with Charm, I got ready to cook.

As I began to cook breakfast, I remembered that I left my bag in the truck. "Jerri, I left my bag in the truck last night. Can you please go get it?"

"The truck is not here. I'll get it for you later."

"What do you mean 'the truck is not here'? My bag is in the truck and it's not here?" The smoke began to come out of my ears as I scrambled the eggs. "So where is the truck, Jerri?" I had already figured the whole thing out—Emmet was outside waiting on Jerri earlier. For whatever reason, Jerri decided to let Shitara use his truck, but he was trying to be slick about the entire thing.

"I got to go pick it up in a minute," he said.

"You didn't answer the question, Mr. Hopkins." By now, fire was coming out of my mouth. His dumb ass wouldn't just say, "I let Shitara use the truck."

"So, Jerri, where is the truck?"

"*Why?*"

"Please don't show off for Emmet please."

"What's the big deal? Call Ivan if you need to go somewhere, baby."

"Don't 'baby' me, Jerri. So now you provide bitches with rides, too. I'm so sick of this bullshit; you need to buy the bitch a car. You think I don't know you take that ho to work every day—now she using the car to get her hair done."

"Neshela, you tripping, baby."

"Tripping! No, I'm not tripping. You got me fucked up. You got this bitch riding around with my shit in the car."

"You tripping," he said. "Look, I only let her use the car because I was trying to rush back home to your ass so I didn't have to hear your mouth about taking too long."

"Jerri, whatever. Do me a favor: you keep my shopping money for the month an' buy your baby mom a car 'cause it really doesn't make much sense that I spend g's at the mall and this ho don't have a car. So do me a favor and buy her a car with the money that I shop with."

"Yo, shut up!" he yelled.

"Who the fuck do you think you talking to?"

"*Shut* the fuck up, Neshela!"

"Jerri, I ain't that bitch and I ain't from Newark, so I don't give a fuck about who you think you are. You got a bitch riding around with my shit in the car. What the hell is this? As a matter of fact, call her and go get my shit."

"Yo, she'll be done in a minute."

"You got fifteen minutes to get my stuff or I'm going to call her and tell her to bring my shit. I'm calling Ivan. I'm going home."

"Going home for what? Here you go again! Go home then—you really showing your ass. I'm not going to stop you. If you want to leave, leave. Whatever!"

"Jerri, one thing that I'm not is a fool. You are still fucking her, Jerri!"

"What Shela? Girl, you stupid. Whatever."

"You nasty motherfucker! I'm pregnant and you fucking bitches!"

"You bugging, Shela. I'm going to get your shit right now."

"You got fifteen minutes. And I mean it, you nasty bastard."

A woman's instinct never lies. For as long as I had been fucking with Jerri, he never let Shitara take a car. It's something fishy about this whole thing. I am good at figuring shit out. I knew at this point that it's something going on. I called Continental to book a flight and Ivan to take me to the airport. It was time to go. Seventeen minutes had passed, Jerri wasn't back yet, nor had he called, so you already know I began to dial Shitara's number.

"Hello, this is Neshela," I said when she picked up.

"This is who?"

"This is Neshela, J's girlfriend."

"J's who?"

"J's girlfriend, or should I say, J's other baby momma. You know, the chick from Miami."

"Oh, the girl from the car, I know. How are you? What do you want?"

"You got the truck and my bags. I need my things; can you drop them by the house?"

"Wait, this is J calling me. You said baby momma? You pregnant? Hold on." A few seconds passed before she was back. "Hello, Niyshe."

"It's Neshela."

"So you're pregnant?" she asked again.

"Yes, for the second time—wait, this is J calling me. In fact, I just need my shit. Can you drop it off?"

"Well, he said he was coming to get it. I told J I was on the phone with you."

"Okay, well, let me see what he wants." I hung up with Shitara and picked up Jerri's call.

"Neshela, I'm on my way," he said. "I'm getting your stuff right now; you didn't have to call her."

"Whatever, Jerri, just bring me my stuff back," I said, and I hung up. I needed a break from this shit. I needed to return to Miami.

Chapter 16

Leaving New Jersey

It was time to gain some stability in my life. I had been flying back and forth between Miami and New Jersey. I had no structure in my life. I was floating and high off love, and that high was low. It was time for me to sit down and analyze my life again.

When I started dating Jerri, I was a mortgage broker and the director of a nonprofit organization, Good Girls for Life, Inc. I made most of my money as a broker, but most of my deals came from my ex-boyfriend Christopher. When Jerri found out that Christopher was my ex, he asked me how much money I made with Christopher each month. I told him about three thousand dollars. He told me to end my business affairs with Christopher and that my allowance would cover my monthly bills. It sounded good at first, but now I realized how much I depended on him. I always had my own and was very independent. I was better than your average twenty-four-year-old; I owned my own home and drove a luxury car. I was also a full-time student at a local college, and while in New Jersey, I attended online classes. I am not your average depend-on-a-nigga type of chick; I just got caught up. I was fueled by love; love kept me driven. Love was my gasoline and I had just run out. Now it's time to get my shit together.

The next few weeks were difficult. Jerri continued putting money into my PNC account. I wouldn't take any calls from him, so he'd call my mother to check on me. I was back in Miami. I had to give myself some time to figure things out. I didn't need him to cloud my judgment. I needed to stay focused on getting my shit together. Jerri was charming, he knew exactly what to do to get to me, but I had to stay focused.

Ironically, a week after I returned to Miami, I received a call from Mrs. Blackmen, the HR director of World Yachting. She called to offer me the executive assistant position. *Damn, shit can't be any worse!* I had to inform her that I was no longer living in New Jersey and couldn't accept the position. She then informed me that the position was based out of their Fort Lauderdale, Florida location. However, if I accepted the position I would have to travel to New York twice a month. She offered me a salary of fifty thousand and an office suite that overlooked downtown Fort Lauderdale. I accepted the position—I was the executive assistant to the vice president of World Yachting. I was getting my swagger back just in time for New Year's.

It's New Year's Eve, and I was alone. Allen called and asked if I had any plans. I didn't, and I didn't bother to act like I did.

"Hey, Allen. I'm just lying in the bed, watching time pass. I am supposed to be in Denver, skiing, but that didn't happen."

"Well, I'm going to Hard Rock tonight. Let me know if you want to go. I'll pick you up if that's okay."

"I'll call you. Talk to you later."

A minute later, the phone rang again; it's Liz this time.

"Girl, what up! It 2006, we'll be twenty-five this year! What you doing tonight?"

"Shut up with that twenty-five shit. I'm twenty-four, chick. I'm not doing anything, just watching time pass."

"What's wrong? How are you feeling?"

"I'm good, I guess"

"You talk to J?"

"No, he hasn't called and I'm not calling him. But you know who did call?"

"Who?"

"Allen," I said.

"Allen, who is that?"

"The dude we met on the beach—the one that we had dinner with."

"Oh, the one that you said was corny."

"Yeah, him."

"So what's up with him?" she asked.

"He asked me to go to Hard Rock tonight. I need to go to church."

"Girl, you should go with him. You need to get out the house"

"Liz, did you forget that I'm pregnant? I'm not going out with any nigga."

"Shit, I didn't say fuck him. I say go out. I wonder what J's doing"

"I don't, fuck him! Anyway, I'm going to sleep. I'll talk to you later, girl."

"Call me if you want to get out."

It was around 11:00 PM when the phone rang and woke me up. It's Allen, asking if I was ready.

"What?" I asked, still half asleep.

"We're going to Hard Rock, right?"

"Yeah, sure I'll meet you at Dunkin Donuts off 595 and 136th Avenue. Give me twenty minutes." I left my car at Dunkin Donuts and went to Hard Rock Cafe with Allen. I was just there physically, 'cause mentally I was in another world until my cell phone rang:

> *I ain't neva had nobody show me all the things that you done showed me*
> *And the special way I feel when you hold me*
> *We gon' always be together, baby, that's what you told me*
> *And I believe it ('cause I ain't neva had nobody do me like u)*

It's Jerri. I couldn't answer it. I didn't need him questioning me. He called four times; finally, he decided to leave a voice mail. I didn't bother to call him back until the following day. Allen and I was out all night. As soon as I walked in the house, I checked my voice mail. The first message was at 12:03 AM: "Happy New Year's, baby. I love you. Call me back." Second message, 12:11 AM: "Neshela, where are you? I'm trying to call you. I guess you're at church. Call me when you get home." Third message, 2:40 AM: "Damn, bitch. I know you see me calling you. Where you at—you pregnant and running the street."

This dude really had a control problem; I don't know who he thought he was talking to. The following day, when I returned his call, he's calm. We talked for a while, and we slept on the phone like old times. But things were different between us; we weren't the same. I began to spend more time with the new dude, Allen. It took a few weeks, but I finally came clean about my relationship with Jerri. I told him enough so that he understood that I was not looking for anything more than a friendship. I failed to mention that I was pregnant. I didn't think it was important yet.

Chapter 17

We Gotta Make It Work

I guess Jerri had an epiphany. I was at work when he called. "Baby I need to talk to you," he said.

"Okay, what's up?"

"Neshela, we need to figure this whole thing out."

"Jerri, what are you talking about?"

"Neshela, we're pregnant and we're falling apart. You don't ever come home anymore."

"Home! I'm home, Jerri. New Jersey is *your* home; I just live there part-time with you. Besides it only been a few weeks."

"Neshela, stop. I'm serious. You and your fucking mouth. I'm trying to talk to you. We don't even talk anymore. I miss you, Shela. Come home."

"I got a job, Jerri. I have to work!"

"Just take a few days off and come home. I need to see you. I love you. Call me when you get off."

"I'll call you. I love you too." I booked a flight for Jersey on Friday. Allen dropped me to the airport and Ivan picked me up. I went straight to the house, where Jerri was awaiting my arrival. I caught him by surprise—I took an earlier flight into Newark. I walked in the door; he was sitting on the couch. I could hear him counting money. Then I heard him cock the gun back

"Jerri, it's me!"

His eyes lit up when I made contact with him at the end of the hallway. "You almost got a hole in you, girl."

"Whatever, you ain't gon' shoot nobody."

"Damn, you're here early, baby. What do you want to do today?"

"Nothing, really."

"How are you feeling?"

"I'm good. Let's go to Essex County Airport," I said.

"You want to fly today? Okay, call and see if they have something available around 3:00 PM."

"I will. Did you eat yet?"

"No."

"Get dressed. Let's go to Toscani."

"You want go fuck with the Italians?"

"Yeah, fool. Let's go, I'm hungry!"

"I was going to take you to Chin Chin," he said.

"Okay baby, that's fine. Can you bring my bags up? I told Ivan to leave them downstairs."

"You brought bags?"

"Yes. I took all my clothes when I left last time, Jerri."

"Why did you bring bags? I thought we were going shopping."

"We can still go shopping tomorrow. I want to go eat and fly today, please."

"Okay baby, there something on the table for you." There's twenty-four white long-stemmed roses set on the table, with a gift bag that contained bottle of Mrs. Dior.

This weekend was like old times. As we lay on the bed reminiscing on the past months, I would go through withdrawal when he wasn't around. A part of me needed him. This trip was the start of a new beginning for us. It is something about this dude that kept me coming back. My job didn't demand much; therefore, I was usually on the phone talking to Jerri and Allen for most of the day. As Jerri and

I began to rebuild our relationship, I continued talking to Allen. He was cool, I guess, or more—so he's something to do when I was in Miami. We had lunch on a regular basis. He owned a beauty salon, a beauty supply store, and a dollar store, so he was always available. We went out often when I was in town. He was fully aware of my rocky relationship with Jerri. He had just got out of a relationship, so he wasn't looking for much. Besides, I knew my belly would be showing soon.

Friday after work, I boarded a flight to Newark. Jerri planned a trip for us to Atlantic City. He invited his friend Husa and his wife, Chanel. We spent the weekend attending shows—the O'Jays, the Levert's, Keith Sweat, Bell Biv DeVoe, and several others. We jammed the night away; we had a fucking ball. We rocked back and forth, singing to each other.

"There you go telling me no again." Keith Sweat had the crowed rocking. It had to be one of the best shows I've ever seen; his old ass was jamming. During intermission, some shit popped off. I don't know the details. I just knew some dude came to our row asking to speak with J. Jerri was missing for about twenty minutes. The crazy part about the whole thing was that my cell phone was in his pocket. When he returned, Bell Biv DeVoe was performing, and Jerri said, "Let's go."

"What wrong with you?" I asked.

"Who the fuck is Allen?"

"Why?" It was about to be a heated debate, but Bobby Brown appeared on the stage, acting like a fool. Our attentions quickly changed to Bobby, who had just taken over the show, and they couldn't get him to stop.

When the show ended, we returned to our room, and Jerri started in on me again. "Who is Allen, Neshela?"

"What are you talking about? You're bugging."

The Slap came a few second later; my mouth dropped. Jerri had never put his hands on me. I went after him, blow after blow; it took everything for him to hold me down. He had me fucked up. There is no way I was going to let him get away with hitting me. When he let me up, I picked up the iron and threw it at him. Then came the coffee pot, shoes—whatever I could pick up, I threw it right at him. I shouted, "The next time you hit me I'll be sending your baldheaded-ass mother a black dress. Have you lost your fucking mind, bitch-ass nigga? Don't you ever put your fucking hands on me, ever!"

"Calm down! I didn't even hit you, I slapped you. You're overreacting, baby. Come here."

"*Fuck you!*" I screamed.

"Come here, Neshela. Come here, baby. I'm sorry, baby. You need to call that nigga an' tell him don't call your number no more."

"What are you talking about?"

"Some nigga text your phone, talking about he miss you."

"Maybe he has the wrong number."

"Don't play with me, bitch. Make the call then."

"No problem." I dialed Allen's number. "Hello. Allen, this is Neshela. You text my phone 'I miss you.' What's up with that?"

Allen was fully aware of my situation. "My bad, baby girl. I was trying to text my girl. I know you got a man; I wouldn't do that."

"Okay, talk to you later."

"Bye."

I hung up and looked at Jerri. "I told you so. I don't even talk to that dude."

"Whatever. Call Sprint and change your number tomorrow."

"Whatever, I'm not changing my number again. You change your number."

"No problem, you just follow my lead."

He made love to me until I feel asleep. The following day we went to Ripley's Believe It or Not. Husa and Jerri danced away on the dance-off game; it was so funny. Chanel and I laughed our asses off—two big grown men dancing, jumping up and down. I recorded it on my cell phone; it was video worth having. As we walked the pier we noticed a psychic's sign. We dared Husa and Chanel to go in. Chanel quickly said no way, and Husa followed her lead. Then they dared us, but we were up for it. We went in one at a time. Jerri went first, then I went, then we went together. The psychic looked at me and said, "You're with child?"

"Yes, I'm pregnant." I answered. Jerri and I looked at each other.

"You're having twins, a girl and a boy."

Jerri and I looked at each other again. "No, not twins."

"Yes, twins."

This lady's crazy. That's all I could think. *I don't need no twins; is she out of her mind?*

She looked Jerri in the eye and said, "You will be the father of three children. Be careful, there's an evil spirit around you. You think she's your friend, you have known her for a few years. She discusses your business with your enemies; be watchful of her."

We both turned and looked at each other, "Monique!"

"You read my mind," we giggled.

As she handed me a blue stone she stated, "Keep this close to you. I wish you the best. By the way, I see numbers around you. Did you change your address or phone number recently?"

"No," I answered quickly.

"I see a change in numbers. Act quickly, it is for the best."

Jerri and I exited the small room with puzzled looks on our faces. The following day, we both changed our numbers.

Before we could leave Atlantic City, we had more drama. Jerri was checking his voice mail—four messages, all from Shitara. She always ruined my mood.

"I heard you and your country-ass bitch are in Atlantic City. You can tell her to stop playing on my phone. I don't care about where y'all at!"

Jerri played the voice mail on speakerphone, so that I could hear just how stupid she sounded.

"You in AC with a bitch an' your daughter need milk."

It was obvious that someone called to inform Shitara that Jerri and I was in Atlantic City, but she had it all wrong if she thought for a second it was me calling her phone. I always looked down on her; she was trash to me, a project chick, a rat. On our ride home, she called to say some slick shit, and you already know I acted like an ass because of the voice messages that she left on Jerri's voice mail. Jerri hated when I acted out in front of people. I have one of those mouths that would make you not like me if you don't know me already. I spat fire out of my mouth; my words cut deep. I can be a true ass at times. In fact, Chanel asked me, "What's wrong with his baby momma, she ugly or something?"

"She's just black and stupid as fuck. She's a silly-ass little girl, always playing kid games. Her shit gets on my nerves. It's always something with her!" I bitched. Chanel just looked at me; she could tell that Shitara did a good job at pissing me off.

Chapter 18

Too Good to Be True

Things continued to go well between Jerri and me. I found out that I was pregnant with twins, just as the psychic said. We were not sure of their sexes, but we decided their names would be Jerri and Jadior, whether they were girls or boys. We were happier than ever. Of course, we had our ups and downs, but I couldn't imagine life without him. He's my man, and I planned to love him forever, and nothing mattered anymore, not the drugs, the lifestyle, or the consequences. As long as we had each other, we'd make it through anything. There was nothing that I wouldn't do for him; he was my everything. I couldn't see myself without Jerri.

It was time to cut Allen off. My belly was beginning to show, and so I was trying to avoid seeing him but he made it hard. He offered to take me to lunch for the entire week. I came up with excuse after excuse. Besides, Jerri was coming to town this weekend. I really didn't need Allen calling my phone again. I continued to ignore his calls. I was sure that he would get the point sooner or later. I had to get ready for the weekend.

I had the entire weekend planned out; I booked a room at the Shore Club. I laid white rose petals all over the suite. I placed a bottle of Patron on ice and lit the candles. Then I rushed to the airport to pick up Jerri. We greeted each other with hugs and kisses. By the time we reached the car, Jerri's phone was ringing on full blast.

"Who is that?" I asked.

"You already know."

"Here we go again. Answer it; maybe something wrong."

Jerri rolled his eyes and answered his phone. "Hello … Yes, Shitara I made it here … Look, you know where I'm at. Don't keep callin' my phone, yo. Call my brother if Charm needs anything. I'll be back Sunday. Bye."

"What did she want?" I asked when he hung up.

"Nothing, really."

"Nothing really? Y'all a little friendly! Now she is checking on you. That is funny." I was not going to let this shit bother me; God knows I didn't care.

When we got to the room, Jerri's mouth dropped; it's breathtaking. The ocean view, the candles, the roses—it was beautiful. He kissed me all over and we made love until sunrise. I didn't want to go anywhere. It is just something about being with him; I never wanted to leave his side.

On Saturday when we finally awoke, we went shopping on Lincoln road. I made dinner reservations at Nikki Beach, one of the sexy spots on South Beach. We had dinner in a private bungalow that sat on the beach. The moon was bright and white. We watched the ocean move back in forth to the rhythm of the music. The following day, we attended my girlfriend's Kay, daughter's birthday party. We didn't stay for long; we just showed our faces. I talked Jerri into staying until Monday, so we decided to spend our last night relaxing.

On the way home, Jerri's cell phone died, and he needed to make some calls. He had to make sure that his runner collected all the money for the streets and had a final count for the day. It was too late to find a charger, and the Nextel store was already closed. So I stopped by my homegirl Nikki's house. She had the same Nextel as Jerri. While I went in the house to charge the phone, Jerri sat in the car. After about ten minutes I pressed the power-on button. His missed-text alerts began to come in. The first was a message from Shitara. It read, "I love you and I will be by your side though the whole thing I want to make this work."

What the fuck is she talking about? I pressed the talk button. I didn't give her a chance to say anything. "Shitara, this is Neshela. You just text J?"

"Hey, Neshela. I want to talk to you, but I'm on the phone with my brother. He's in jail. Can you call me back in ten minutes?"

"Okay, answer the phone!" I watched the clock for ten minutes straight. I was dying to hear what she had to say. It was exactly ten minutes when I called her back. She picked up right away; I guess we both wanted to talk to each other.

"Shitara, this is Neshela again," I said when she answered.

"I know."

"You just text J, and I don't understand."

"Well me and J decided to work things out. That's why he went down there this weekend—to tell you."

"Oh, really? He came to tell me *what*? Ha ha. That funny. Is that what he told you?"

"No, that's what it is. I'm going to be with him; we will work through this. I will learn to accept your child," she said.

"I'm a little confused here!"

"Well, J came back home on Wednesday."

"*Home?*"

"He told me he wants his family back; he told me that

you are not in Jersey anymore, and ya'll were not together. He told me he wants his family back and I'm willing to give it to him."

"I don't know where to begin." I said. "I'm going to call you from my cell phone; I have to get in the car." I got in the car, but I didn't say a word to Jerri. I had to play it cool. I didn't know her intentions, and I wanted to hear the entire story first.

"Baby, what wrong with you?" Jerri asked, noticing my silence.

"Nothing. Shitara text you about working through things. What the fuck is that about?"

"That bitch crazy. She called me, crying, on the phone a few days ago, about she want to make it work."

"Oh really, so what did you say"?

"I didn't say anything. I hung up on her; she crazy. I don't know what that bitch going through."

"Yeah, anyway, Liz and her dude is having problems; I have to call her back," I said. I was really calling Shitara. She picked up right away. "Hello, can you talk?"

"Yeah, I'm with J, but I can talk. Go ahead tell me the story, Liz." That basically meant that I couldn't respond but I could listen, and she caught on; she told it all. "I knew every time that you were in Jersey; I live right around the corner from the house on Sixth Street. Jerri and I was happy until you came about; in fact, we lived together."

"What when was this?"

"You ruined my happy home, and now I want it back."

"I don't understand. What are you talking about?" I wanted to say more, but I couldn't. Jerri was still sitting next to me.

"Look, I don't know where you came from, but out of nowhere, Jerri moved out of our house to the house on

Sixth Street. Things were fine between us; in fact we had just came back from a family vacation to Jamaica."

"Jamaica!"

"Yes, Jamaica. A month or so after the trip, he starts acting funny. He spent the weekend out, then the next week he moved out. With no explanation, he just moved out. It took me a minute to figure the whole thing out, but it was you."

"Me! What do you mean?"

"You took him from me!" she said.

This shit was getting ridiculous. Seventeen minutes and twenty-three seconds of her going on and on, like we were friends and I stole her man. In my mind, I was thinking, *This bitch is crazy. Shit, I don't know her and I ain't takin' shit from her.* I didn't want Jerri to know yet, so I had to keep my cool. When we arrived at the house, I told Jerri that Liz really needed to talk 'cause her and Mike got in a big fight, so I was going to stay outside to talk to her. I finally had my chance to respond.

"Do you approve of how he did me that night; do you think that was right?" Shitara asked.

"No, I don't think that it was right," I said, "but it appeared that you were going to throw a bottle at the window where I was sitting, so he did what he was supposed to do—protect me. You chose to fuck him after that, so you approved of it. Jerri would have never—Look, Shitara. I didn't take him from you. In fact, Jerri told me you were his sidekick that just happened to get pregnant. He told me that he was with Jason's mother, and he was fucking you every now and then. You both were pregnant at the same time, unfortunately, Jason's mother miscarried after she found out about you. He talks about her more than anything. All I know about you is that you're the project chick that he fucking with and your actions constantly prove that."

"My actions don't make you think that we are still fucking."

"No, your actions make me think that you were stupid. I am no secret, he doesn't hide me, and when you did that child-support shit, that validated your stupidity. As much as Jerri does for you and Charm, you have some nerves to put him on child-support."

"J said Charm wasn't his. That's why I did that; I wasn't going to follow through with it."

"Charm looks just like Jerri. He wouldn't say that—he love that baby to death."

"You obviously don't know J."

"You're right, I don't know J. I know Jerri Hopkins, the man that I sleep with. The man I love."

"I've caught J with so many girls—you just don't know. But I love him and I'm going to be with him, and we'll overcome this."

This bitch is crazy, I thought. *The dick was good, but my God! I can't deal with this; I am three months pregnant.* "So what are you saying, Shitara?"

"I'm saying that I'm willing to accept your baby and I will be with J. He told me everything. I know everything about y'all. He came over here begging me to be with him; I was done with him."

It's time for Jerri Hopkins to be a part of this conversation. I put the phone on mute as I walked in the house. I quickly informed Jerri that I was not talking to Liz; it was really Shitara.

"We have been talking for over one hour and a half. I want clarity about everything, so it is time for truth. Shitara, you're on speakerphone, and Jerri can hear everything. You said he told you everything; what do you mean? And 'accept my baby,' what does that mean?"

"I'll accept your child because he said it's his. He has two children and that's it."

"My babies. I'm having twins, Shitara."

"Twins!"

"Oh, I guess he failed to mention that. He has four children, not two."

"He has three children. Jason is not his son!"

Wow, so much shit made sense now. It's clear that Shitara didn't like Jason or his mother—she wanted to be Jerri's only baby momma. She stated that she didn't like how Jerri spent so much time with Jason. "Jason is his son if he says Jason is his son!" I insisted.

"Jason is not his son, and I'm sick of him playing dad to everybody but Charm."

"Look, I don't want to talk about that. Jerri is sitting right here. We need to get shit clear; it appears that someone failed to mention a lot of things. I guess he didn't tell you that I'm moving to Jersey in April." I looked at Jerri. "I guess you don't tell her a lot of things. So tell me, Jerri. Tell me what's going on."

"Hang up the phone. She's lying; I ain't going over anywhere," Jerri said.

"Now I'm lying, J? You didn't sleep over here? We didn't have sex? You didn't tell me you want your family back? I'm lying? I'm lying, J. You ain't shit! You get in front of her and get amnesia. I see. *Fuck You, J! Fuck you!*" Her voice began to crack. I could hear the pain through the phone. I can't imagine how she felt—he denied her again for me. After two hours of talking to her, I felt sorry for her. She was a victim of love. I guess we both were.

She took a deep breath, but her voice was still cracking.

"J, your daughter has a doctor's appointment at 9:00 tomorrow morning; I guess you're not going to be here to take her."

"I told you to call Red if Charm needs anything," Jerri said.

"Yeah. You told me you love me; you told me you were going to tell her; you told me you would be back on Sunday. J, you tell me anything."

"I got to go," he said and hung up the phone, not giving her a chance to say a word.

"So tell me, Jerri, what's going on? What going on, baby?" I asked.

"Shela, she lying. I ain't go over there." He said it calm and slow—I knew he's lying. I looked at him from the corner of my eye.

"I'm not her; don't sit here and lie in my face. Don't you dare disrespect me. It's time to be real with yourself and time to be real with me. I want to know, Jerri. I need to know the truth. I respect the truth and I deserve it."

"Shela, I love you to death and you know it. You are really my better half, but after the abortion I thought we were over. I started fucking Shitara. It only happened a few times, but I didn't want her; that's why I flew to Miami the week when you weren't taking my calls."

"Jerri, it's February. The abortion was November ninth. The IVF was on December fourteenth. Please help me understand. What the fuck are you talking about?"

"Baby, listen. I don't know how to say it."

"Just say it!"

"Shela, I don't want to lose you; I love the shit out of you! I never loved anyone the way I love you. You're my wife and I mean that."

"So what is Shitara talking about, Jerri?"

"I don't know."

"Jerri, please just tell me, baby."

"Shela, I love her too, and I can't imagine her with anyone else. In fact, I can't allow her to be with anyone else."

"*What?*"

"I told you I didn't know how to say it. I love you both for so many different reasons. Shela, she could never be you, even if she tried. But you can't be her, either," he said. For the first time, he's being honest, and it was killing me inside. I had been living a lie for eight months. We sat down and made all of these plans while he was being unfaithful.

"Shela, I'm like her father; she needs me, yo."

"What the fuck are you talking about? Is that the excuse that you're going to use for fucking her, Jerri? *I'm like her father; she needs me!* What the fuck is that supposed to mean to me?" I was so hurt I didn't want to be near him. "I have to leave."

"You can't leave me," he said.

"I'm gone. You can take your flight; go be with your family. Beside, Charm has a doctor appointment in the morning. If you take the early flight you can make it in time. I'm going to sleep at my parents' house."

"You can't leave me, Shela. You can't."

"Watch me, Jerri. Watch me!"

He lay in the bed as if I was not going to leave. It's not until I put my shoes on that he jumped up. "Where you think you going?"

"Save that shit. I'm gone. I can't deal with this—I won't deal this!"

He jumped in front of me and grabbed my arms. "You're not going anywhere."

"Let me go, Jerri. Let me go now." I just wanted to leave, and that's the plan. Until Jerri threw me on the bed.

"You're not going anywhere. Let's talk about it. We can fix it, Shela. I love you."

"You tripping, Jerri. You don't love me. Get off of me. I got to go."

"Please don't go. I'm sorry!"

"I can't do this, Jerri. I can't do this anymore—the back and forth, the stress, it ain't worth it. I'd rather be alone."

"What do you mean? Remember when you said you would never leave, you said you'll never have another abortion?"

"I didn't think it would be this bad, Jerri. I never thought it be this way."

"If you kill my babies; I'ma kill you!"

"I hate you, Jerri Hopkins! *I hate you!*" I crawled in the bed and rocked myself to sleep. I couldn't cry. I wouldn't allow myself to—God knows I wanted to. Being hurt wasn't part of the plan, and we had just crossed the line between love and hate. I never thought this day would come. I thought the truth was something that I could take, but it was too much for me. I was hurt and I wasn't trying to hide it. He broke my heart. For the first time in our relationship, I wanted to be lied to.

I woke up to breakfast in bed, hoping it was all a bad dream. But it wasn't. While brushing my teeth, I noticed the black-and-blue bruises from the night before on my arms. I looked hopelessly in the mirror; the tears wouldn't stop flowing. *Here I go again,* I thought. *I'm three months pregnant with twins from a dope boy whose baby mom is on call, willing and waiting. What am I going to do?*

I wanted him to go home so bad, but he wouldn't leave Miami. So on Tuesday I decided to go to work. I refused to sit in the house with him. When I returned home from work, there was bags all over the floor, just like when we first met. I walked over them as if they were not there, but the dozen white roses caught my eyes. There was a small card that read "Let's start over."

That evening, we had dinner at a hibachi restaurant. Shitara called my cell phone; I left the table to talk to her. She sounded hopeless and it was obvious that she had no one to call, no one to share the embarrassment, no one to understand the pain. While pressed against the stall in the women's restroom, I listened to her cry and for the first time, a part of me understood her. After eight minutes, I had to go. I knew Jerri would be wondering who I was talking to and what's taking so long. Therefore, I had to end the call.

"Shitara, I have to go; we're at dinner. I went to the restroom so that I could talk to you. I know Jerri is wondering what's taking me so long."

"Neshela, I'm sorry to bug you. I just don't have anyone else to call; my girls told me to leave him."

"Yeah, I know how that is! He loves you; it'll be okay. Good luck." It is odd telling the other chick that your man loves her, but it was the truth and I knew it. I couldn't let it bother me.

It wasn't until Thursday that Jerri finally decided to go back to Newark. For some reason, he thought our relationship was on the way to a new start, and that everything was going to work out. But at this point, I was debating another abortion. I didn't want any parts of him. I was truly fed up this time. I loved him, but I was not willing to deal with the bullshit—and I knew Shitara wasn't going anywhere. She was too weak and too needy to let go of Jerri. It didn't matter how many times he disrespected her to prove a point to me, she was happy with just having a piece of him. Me, on the other hand, I am just too good to be second—or any part of a love triangle. I'm not the type to share, so this wasn't going to work.

Jerri always had a way of making things work in his favor. Right before he left, he told me of his plans to take me to Hawaii—he had a brother that lived in Kuhio, an island of Oahu, Hawaii. How could I say no to this?

Chapter 19

Problems

It seemed that everyone's "happily ever after" wasn't so happy these days. Mimi and Quan were having their share of drama. I don't know what exactly was going on between the two of them. I just knew that she needed someone to lean on, and I made myself available. Mimi flew into Ft. Lauderdale International airport; it was a week of girl talk and just plain old catching up. We had a ball in the mist of our uncertainty; we always made the best of our time together. We tried hard to laugh and have fun, spending as little time as possible thinking about our problems. Like me, Mimi was pregnant and unsure about her relationship and its direction. Coming to Miami gave her the opportunity to see things clearly; she needed the break. By the time she left Miami, she wrote Quan a book about their relationship. It was her form of therapy. When she finished the book she returned to Jersey, and they decided to work things out.

For me, on the other hand, things were going downhill. Nothing was the same between Jerri and me. I had lost all respect for him; I was done. I called him one night and he didn't answer. For as long as we had been together, he always answered the phone or called back within minutes. But this night was different; he didn't answer, and I, like any pregnant woman, began to worry. I called Abdul; he said that he hadn't spoken with him and that he would call me right back. I called Quan and Mack—no one had heard from him. Abdul called me back to tell me that Jerri had been arrested earlier that day and was still in jail. Abdul said that Jerri was fine and not to worry, and he was on his way to bail him out. Then the funniest thing happened when Quan called back. He said that Jerri was okay, not to worry, and that Jerri will be calling me any minute.

I felt that someone was lying, so I called my homey at Sprint/Nextel and asked him to print everyone's call log for the day. He worked in billing, so he was able to get into their accounts and get me all of their call logs within a couple of hours. Just like I thought everyone was lying: Jerri, Abdul, Mack, and Quan. —especially Abdul and Jerri. Both of Jerri's cell phones were on blast that day and night. I even went a step further and called all five precincts in Newark looking for Jerri. No one had been booked by the name Jerri O. Hopkins. The one thing that I am good at is dissecting lies, and I had just pulled this one apart. Now that I knew the lie, figuring out the truth is a piece of cake.

When Jerri called the following morning, he told me a wonderful story about being pulled over. I acted all concerned, just as he thought I would. But at the end of his detailed story, I asked, "Baby, what precinct pulled you over; was it in Newark?" And of course he replied, "Precinct three. Why you trying to be funny?"

"You fucking lair," I said, and when I finished cussing him out, I just hung up in his face. He had to feel so stupid. The one thing I hate is being lied to, especially by the people I love. I know Jerri very well; he lied because he was with someone. We slept on the phone just about every night when I wasn't in town, and he always answered my calls, but things began to change. This stunt was the start of a new beginning. Jerri hated being called out, so the very next day he put two g's in my PNC account and sent me a text, "Sorry for lying go shopping I put 2 gs in your account." By now I was sick of the "I'm sorry" and the make-up shopping sprees. Two g's; I felt like he's selling me short. What was I going to do with two g's?

The next few weeks went fine; everything appeared to be normal. I woke up around 3:00 AM, and my stomach was killing me. It was the worst pain that I had ever felt. I got up and went to the bathroom. Blood was dripping down my legs! I immediately called Jerri, and then my doctor, who instructed me to go to the emergency room, and I did as I was told. I continued to call Jerri, but, to my surprise, he didn't answer. I called three more times, and finally, the third call, he answers, *"What?"*

"Who the fuck are you talking to? I'm bleeding."

"Where are you?"

"On the way to the hospital. The doctor told me to go to the hospital."

"I'll call you back let me get up."

"What? You gon' call me back!" I couldn't believe him.

"Yeah. I'll call you back; I'm sleeping."

I hung up the phone and press the power-off button.

The one thing I have is good sense, and it's obvious that someone was lying next to him. I turned my cell phone off and didn't accept any calls from anyone. I stayed in the hospital for two days. Thanks to God, everything turned out to be okay; the twins were fine. My doctor put me on bed rest for one week. When they released me, I didn't even bother to call Jerri. In fact, I stopped calling him. I even had his phone disconnected. There was no point in him having a phone in my name that he didn't answer when I called.

Jerri had four dozen white roses delivered to my house, but that didn't work this time. The week of bed rest allowed me to analyze my situation again. It seemed like just yesterday when everything was great. At one point, I was everything that he wanted, but now things were different. I used to think that he was heaven-sent, but somehow our signals got crossed. It was time for me to move on. I knew that he loved me, but he wasn't ready for all the things that we planned. And I'm hurt again because at this point I knew better. I was just trying to make it work; I was willing to be his wife and the mother of his kids, but I wasn't going to accept him being a part-time man. Therefore, I had to mentally prepare myself for the abortion that I must have.

The next few days would be difficult; I really needed an escape but I had nowhere to go. I decided to call Mimi—I needed a friend that understood my relationship. She's the closest person to the both of us. Jerri would call and tell her stuff, and so would I. She does a good job of helping us understand each other. After I told her of my plans, she said, "Girl, you're crazy. J will kill you! You can't do that, Shela."

"Mimi, fuck J. I'm not going to deal with this. I don't deserve this! I just want to wash my hands of this whole thing."

"Neshela, you don't think for a second that you expect too much?"

"Expect too much? I'm pregnant!"

"So am I."

"You don't understand; I know him, Mimi. I'll be damned if I'm on the way to the hospital and he tell me to call him back. If you think that shit is acceptable, you're crazy too! I'm not going to do this alone Mimi, no way. Imagine me with three kids! What the hell do I look like?"

"Last time I checked, you both decided to do that IVF shit! You should have been sure, Neshela. Look chick, you'll be okay. Those kids are a blessing, and besides, you just had an abortion. It hasn't even been six months yet.

Everything will be okay. I have to cook dinner; Quan is on the way home. I love you, girl."

"Love you too. Talk to you later." I still needed someone to talk to, so I decided to call Liz. She answered the phone and started checking up on me right away. "What's up, Neshela? How are you feeling; you need anything?"

"No, I'm good," I lied.

"What's wrong? I can hear it in your voice; what are you stressing about, girl?"

"Nothing, I'm fine."

"Stop lying. What happened?"

"I want to have an abortion!"

"*What?* I thought you said that—"

"I know what I said, but that was before I found out that J is fucking around. I can't do this shit—*Twins!*"

"Look, girl, I'll support you with whatever you decide, but I can surely think of a better way of wasting seven g's."

"It wasn't a waste! I want to have his baby; I want to be a family; I want it all, Liz, and you know it. But things change, and there's no coming back from some shit. Things haven't been the same for me since that whole Shitara shit a few months ago—he had the nerve to say 'I love you both.'"

"You accepted it then, so what the problem now!"

"I *don't* accept shit; I respect his honesty."

"Girl, all men cheat. Besides, it's his baby mom, the project chick. He gonna always fuck that ho and you know it. Therefore, I don't see the problem."

"You don't see the problem? All men don't cheat. Weak women allow men to cheat on them. If I wasn't pregnant, I wouldn't be with J to save my life, and you know it."

"I hear you, but I'm starting to think that you have lost your mind. One day you want one thing, the next day you want something else. *What* do you want? I mean he does everything for you; he gives you whatever you want; he spoils you to death and treats you like a queen most of the time. Come on girl, stop playing! When you find Mr. Perfect I want to meet his brother. All I know is that he's going to kill you if you tell him that you're going to have another abortion. Maybe you should think about it. Remember, I'm here for you, no matter what."

"Yeah, you're right. I'm going to think about it. I'll call you later."

"Okay, bye."

Chapter 20

New Shit

My job was ending; the company was relocating to Dubai, and God knows I wasn't going. I was just starting to love my position as the executive assistant to one of the richest men in the United States. Who would have ever imagined! I set up meetings with some of the most elite individuals, such as Donald Trump, Andrew Fakes, and so many others. Hood rich and wealthy was two completely different things. I grew up having the finer things in life. We were definitely upper-middle class. I remember attending acting and etiquette classes as a child. We had a housekeeper and everything we could ever want for. My mother drove a Benz for most of my life. Even as an adult, I usually got what I wanted. I never fucked with broke niggas. Whether they were athletes, businessmen, or my new category—dope boys, they always had cash or lots of potential. But my boss, it was a different kind of cash. When he told me to book the hall for his engagement party and to buy the ring, I damn near fainted. The ring was $92,989 and the hall, the naked hall, was $85,000. By the time the designer got finished with the perfect engagement party— *not* the wedding, the engagement party—it cost $157,000. That's how I wanted to live; that's what I wanted my life to be like.

It was my last week at work when the receptionist called my desk to inform me that the vice president of Bank of America's commercial real estate division had been asking about me and that he had left his card about a week ago. She said that she had tried to call me a few times, but she thought that I was at the New York office and didn't feel that it was that important.

"The VP of Bank of America left his card for me and you didn't think that it was important?" Seeing that it was my last week, I didn't make a big deal of it. I just picked up the card on my way out. The name on the business card was Okwui Olugbenga, and, surely, his title read, "Vice President of Bank of America, Commercial Real Estate Division," in bold print. His cell number was handwritten on the back of the card: 954-555-9006. Usually I wouldn't call so early, but considering the dumb blonde had the card sitting at her desk for a week, I decided to call. I practiced his name for twenty minutes, hoping not to mess it up.

"Hello," he caught me off guard; he didn't have an accent, so I stumbled

"Hello, my name is Neshela. You left your card with the receptionist for me. How may I help you?"

"Hi, my name is Ok-wu-i. I work on the forty-sixth floor, and I noticed you a few weeks ago. I was wondering if I could take you to lunch sometime."

I wondered if he had the right person—he had to notice the pudge that I was carrying. I'm still pregnant. "You want to take *me* to lunch? Are you sure you have the right person?"

"Yes, I know who I'm talking to; you drive a black Mercedes Benz, right? You're the assistant to Mr. White."

"Yes, I do. And yes, I was. I don't think we've met."

"We haven't."

Oh, hell no! I wasn't trying to meet the stalker on the forty-sixth floor, fuck that title. But after a few days of playing phone tag with Mr. Okwui, we finally met up for lunch. He turned out to be a cool dude, a little cheap, but overall he was a nice guy. He ask me to join him for lunch the following day, but I had plans with Allen. He'd called a few days earlier. I had been avoiding him for a while. Remember when Jerri was in town a few months ago? I basically ignored Allen for the entire weekend.

Allen and I had lunch at Slashes, a Mexican spot near my job. I told him that it was my last day at work and that I had ended my relationship with Jerri. I suggested that we could spend more time together, considering I need someone to sponsor a few meals for the next month or so. I wasn't rushing back into the job market; besides I was making good money doing mortgages at home. At lunch Allen informed me that he saw me at a traffic light a while back, with a male in the car. He then asked if it was Jerri sitting in the passenger seat of my car. *Damn he saw me!* I didn't respond.

While sitting in the house, organizing the hospital bills that I had accumulated during the two pregnancies, I realized that I had too much time on my hands, and that was never a good thing. I was beginning to miss Jerri. Suddenly my cell phone rang it was Allen. He called to offer me a position at one of his offices. "Hey, Neshela. You working yet?" he asked.

"*No!* Why?"

"'Cause I just fired my branch manager, and I need someone to replace her ASAP."

"Oh, really. So what makes you think that I'll be good for the job?"

"Well you are a mortgage broker, and that's really all the

experience that you need—and a little bit of management; I'm sure you got that! So when can you start?"

"When can I start? I never said yes! I enjoy sitting at home, sweetie. I'm not planning to go back to work." I was lying through my teeth, but I wasn't really interested in working for him. Besides I didn't need the money. Jerri was still putting money in my PNC account—not as much as he used to, but considering that I hadn't talked to him in at least three weeks, it was a fair amount. "Look, Allen, I have to think about it. I'll let you know."

"The salary is no cap. I'll give you a thousand dollars a week plus commission to start, and you can still broker all your own loans at the office."

This was starting to sound good. "I'll let you know." I couldn't act all press about a stack a week; it was good money to manage an office full of dumbass niggas. Therefore, I took the job mentally but waited a few days before I told Allen. I thought it was going to be a cakewalk, but I was in for a rude awakening.

The first few days were rough; there was no order in the office, people just did whatever they wanted, and the branch manager was not quite fired yet, so there was a little tension in the office. And everyone knew that Allen liked me. That was no secret, which made things even more difficult because most of the chicks that worked in the office liked him. See, Allen was fine as hell; he stood six foot two inches and weighed 232 pounds of solid muscle, and when he put on a suit—*shit!* So you already know the story, "He only hired her because he fucking her; she probably don't know shit about mortgages." Those two brainless fools didn't even hear me walk in the office. I love to hear how stupid women think. "Good morning," I said pleasantly. It took them a second to respond; they were trying to figure out if I heard them gossiping about me. I was used to people thinking that my body and my beauty took me places, but usually it was really my brain that got me there. My attitude was so fucked up that I needed my brain—my mouth was deadly, so I only used it when I needed to.

Chapter 21

Boom

The following day, I was riding down Flamingo and suddenly, "Boom!" *Fuck!* I'd just wrecked my car; this chick ran right into me. What a day! I spent most of the evening in the ER, laying on a back brace—this had to suck. My phone didn't stop ringing; everyone was calling to check on me. I felt so loved. Allen offered to sit in the ER with me, but I declined. I didn't want to be bothered, nor did I want him to know that I was pregnant.

The doctor came in and informed me that the twins didn't make it. The impact from the crash caused me to have a miscarriage. I left the ER thirteen hours later with two prescriptions—one for the pain and the other for bleeding. After the miscarriage, I felt empty but I was relieved. No one wants to go through that but it's for the best. I was pretty banged up, but surprisingly, my car only had slight damages. It took two days to get it fixed. I was so excited to have my car back that I took the long way home.

While in route, my Pocket PC vibrated. It shocked me because this phone hardly rang. In fact, only a few people had the number. The text read, "From: 8605559367 it used 2 b a time when we couldn't go without talking 2 each other now it's obvious that we don't even care or our egos r 2 big. I still love." A tear rolled down my cheek; I still loved him so much, but it had been at least a month since the last time we'd talked or seen each other. I knew that he was still calling my mother to check on me. My little brother would tell me every now and then. When I arrived at my house, I climbed in the bed and cried myself to sleep, holding the ultrasound of the twins close to my heart.

A week later, Mimi called. "What up, chick?"

"Nothing," she said. "How are you doing?"

"I'm okay. What's going on?"

"You got your car yet, chick?" she asked.

"I've had my car for a week now. It only took the body shop two days to fix it."

"Oh, I thought it was a bad accident."

"It didn't turn out that bad after all; I'm still alive!"

"Okay smart-ass. Anyway, have you talked to J?"

"No, why?"

"No reason, I just asked. Are you going to tell him?"

"No. I'm not calling him, Mimi, and I mean it."

"Well, he called me today and asked me how you were."

"Well he called the wrong person. If he wanted to know how I was, he would have called me," I said. "What did you tell him?"

"The truth!"

"What do you mean?"

"I told him that I haven't talk to you in about a week. I also told him that you were in a bad car accident, and that's it."

"Oh, that probably why he text me a few day ago."

"I just hung up with him a few seconds before I called you. I told him that I would call and check on you and call him back. Let me call him back and tell him you okay."

"Whatever, bye. Stop letting him make you do his dirty work."

"Whatever, chick. I'd do it for you, and you would do it for Quan. Bye."

A few minutes after Mimi called, I received another text from Jerri: "please call we need to talk." I just ignored it. If he had enough time to text me, he had enough time to call. Therefore, I continued with my day. I had a lot of work to do in the office. It was a long day; I had to interview someone for a receptionist position, and the map log was behind, so I had to map about sixty addresses for the street team. I really didn't have time for Jerri and his bullshit. I had to stay focused. I had to live life without him. On top of all the shit I had to do in the office, Allen decided that he wanted to have a mandatory meeting at the Carol City office. I had a little over three hours to get all my work done and interview six people. Call me super woman! I did it.

While in route to the Carol City office, my cell phone rang. To my surprise, it was Jerri. "Hey baby, how are you?"

"Who is this?" I asked. As if I didn't know his voice.

"J."

"Oh, what's up? What do you want?"

"How are you?"

"Fine."

"How are the twins?"

"Dead."

"What?" His voice cracked. "What did you say?"

"I had a miscarriage a week ago."

"I'm sorry I couldn't be there for you. I'm sorry. How are you feeling?"

"Jerri, I'm fine. It's been over a month since we talked."

"Come and see me!" he begged.

"You're funny! Look, the one thing that would have kept us, the one thing—or should I say the two babies—

that would have made us communicate are *dead*. Too bad you're just finding out. I got to go."

"*What?*"

"There's nothing else for us to talk about. Bye." I hung up the phone, not giving him a chance to say a word, and he didn't bother to call back. I held the phone in my hand, hoping he would. About a week after our short conversation, I began to receive a voice mail on a daily basis. It was the chorus of a song. The first few days I ignored it, but on the fourth day I decided to put some thought to it. After about thirty minutes, I couldn't figure it out, so I called Lisa and said, "Hey, I need some help decoding a song."

"Who is it?"

"I'm not sure. Meet me at Target on Stirling Road and University Drive."

"Girl, it better be important!"

"It is. Love you"

"I'll be there in fifteen minutes."

"Thanks." It took us forty minutes to narrow the voice down to Avant or Ginuwine. I decided to call Jerri and ask him who the hell was singing this song. My patience was running short. He answered on the first ring, "I miss you come home."

"Boy, you're crazy. Who sing this song? I can't figure it out."

"I don't know what you're talking about."

"Stop playing. I got Lisa out of her bed; we been try to figure it out. I know that it Ginuwine or Avant. Tell me, please. Target is about to close."

"It Ginuwine. 'Far Away.'" He hung up, and I ran in Target to get the CD. It was number twelve. Lisa and I sat in Target's parking lot and listened to it. I wanted to cry; the song represented us, but we hadn't played this game in so long. I responded with Avant, "4 minutes," the last forty seconds of the song. He had four minutes, and he chose to wait until he was out of time. I was done with Jerri O. Hopkins—it was too late. Besides, Allen offered every-thing that I wanted, stability and security, and I didn't have to worry about the Feds kicking in the door. Of course, I was still madly in love with Jerri, but I had to draw the line. The next few weeks were difficult. Jerri continued to call on a regular basis, and I continue to take his calls and talk to him for long periods of time. One of his calls was touching, "I know I'm not the man for you right now, but I plan to stop this shit in two years. Jason is getting old; I don't want him to do this, Shela, and I really want to stop. I need two years, maybe three. I want to move to Virginia or somewhere."

"Let's move to Atlanta," I said.

"That's too far. Virginia or Maryland; wait on me, Shela. I love you."

"You crazy!"

"I'm serious."

"Yeah, what happened to the truck shit that you were serious about before?"

"Man, Mike be tripping I can't do nothing with him."

"You need to get your GED, Jerri. You have to start some-where, but there is no sense in me preaching to you; you already know what you need to do."

"Don't worry, I'll do it."

"Bye, fool. I love you."

"Love you too."

Two days later, Jerri called to tell me that he got saved; I was so happy for him I wanted to cry.

"Neshela, my mother was just crying. If I had known it would have meant that much to her, I would have been did it."

"Baby, I'm so happy for you. I love so much."

"Just because I got saved?"

"No fool, I love you for so many reasons. I'm happy that you got saved, baby, thank you."

"Yeah, you been asking me to get saved for a minute, but, Shela, I never knew that it would affect my mother that way."

"Jerri, you're her baby, her spitting image, and she's a woman of God, so of course it would affect her. Baby, you have a spot in the kingdom now, you're covered. If anything ever happens, just repent. 'God forgive me for my sins,' and you'll be good."

"Shit, is that it?"

"No, crazy. That's the basics, anyway. I'm at work I have to go." I'm not sure as to what happened; I just know that he stopped calling, so I didn't bother to call him after I didn't hear from him for a week. Beside I was mad that he wouldn't pay the hospital bills that I had accumulated during the two pregnancies.

Chapter 22

Back in Jersey

"What time does your flight land tomorrow?" Mimi asked.

"Don't worry. I'll have Ivan pick me up from the airport. You and Quan have too much to worry about. I'll be there.

"I can't believe that you're only coming up for one day, Neshela"

"Girl, Allen is too insecure about Jerri; I won't do it to him. I kind of like him, so I don't want him to get any thoughts, besides he just gave me the salon. I don't need to fuck this one up, not yet."

"I feel you. Well, I'll see you tomorrow."

"Love you, girl. I'll be there."

"Love you too. Bye." I had a big day ahead of me, but instead of Ivan, my homey Derrick picked me up from the airport. It felt funny being back in Jersey. I had not been to Newark since February, and it was now May. *Wow,* I thought. *I remember when I was here every week. Dirty-ass Newark. Nothing's changed.* Derrick and I went to get a bite to eat from Legal Seafood at Shore Hill mall. After dinner, I ran in Gucci to get the baby a gift, and I couldn't resist buying a pair of heels for myself—okay, maybe three pairs. After the mall, I changed into my outfit for the baby shower. I decided to wear a pair of Gucci sandals with an army green pant set and a pair of Gucci shades and my Gucci bag to match. I walked in the hall, excited to see my friends. Mimi doubted my attendance, so she was surprised to see me when I walked in the hall. She greeted me with a big hug. "Chick, you look good."

"So do you! You're so big and pretty; oh my God! Look at your stomach, Mimi!" I took a quick glance across the room just to spot familiar faces. I saw Doman, Mack, Wesley, and Jennifer; everyone was there.

I could tell that Rachel, Mimi's best friend, didn't notice me. She looked at me out of the corner of her eye but didn't say a word. "Rachel, don't act like you don't know me," I said as I pulled up my shades so she could see my face.

"Neshela, I swear I didn't know that it was you. I seen you when you walked in, looking all Hollywood and shit—bitch, you look good. Who did your make up? Did you lose some weight? You look real nice."

"I know, I'm supposed to!"

"Shut up, girl. Let's get some food." We stood in the line, chitchatting while we waited to be served. It was so nice to see everyone. I sat at the back table next to Wesley and Jennifer with the rest of the crew. We all tripped out making jokes and talking about people as they passed. It felt good hanging out with the crew again. It's been so long. I bent my head down for a second to get my cell phone from my bag; I wanted to call Allen and tell him that I made it.

"There go your corny-ass nigga." It was Wesley's voice, but I wasn't sure who or what he was talking about. I was too busy looking for my cell phone. When I looked up, Jerri was still in front of our table. He spoke to a few people and walked away. We didn't say a word to each other, but in a matter of seconds, Quan appeared at the table and informed me that Jerri wanted to talk to me.

"Quan, I don't have no rap for him. Tell him if he wants

to talk about them hospital bills that he hasn't paid, we can talk."

Quan became the messenger between the two of us. "Neshela, please talk to him. We all make mistakes; he didn't know."

"Quan, he knows. I told him; he knew."

"*Man*. Talk to him for me, Neshela, come on."

"No, Quan. If I was your daughter, would you be saying the same thing?"

Quan just looked at me and walked off; he knew I was right. Therefore, I enjoyed the rest of the evening as if Jerri was not there. The baby shower was lovely; it was a least one hundred and fifty people in attendance. Little Quan was already ready for the world: Gucci, Christian Dior, Neiman Marcus, Saks—there was all type of bags and en-velopes covering the floor of the square reception hall. The night was coming to an end, and my flight was scheduled for 7:40 PM. It was about 5:20, and Rachel asked me to help pass out the thank-you gifts. We split the room in half; I covered one side and she did the other. I had four vases left—one for me, and the remaining vases for the three guys standing near the door. I handed the first vase to the dude standing in front of me, who happened to be Em-met. I didn't know the second guy, and of course Jerri was the third guy. "Here's your thank-you gift from Mimi and Quan."

"Hold it and bring it home for me."

"Sorry, I can't do that. Do you want it or not?"

"Neshela, let me take you to the airport."

"No, thanks."

"I love your bracelet." He was clearly trying to make me talk to him.

"Thanks," I said.

"Where did you get it?"

"My ex bought it for me. It's Channel—Five and a half carats!"

"That's nice. He must really love you."

"I'm sure if he did I wouldn't have five thousand dollars in hospital bills, but anyway, I have to go. Do you want the vase or not?"

"I heard that you're going to Mexico; can I meet you there?"

"It's a free country, do whatever you want!"

"Who's taking you to the airport?"

"Bill is giving me a ride to the airport."

"Shela, let me took you to the airport. We need to talk; I got this song that I want you to hear."

"My stuff is already in Bill's car."

"That's nothing. I'll get it."

"Okay." I gave in. Now I had to tell Quan. *Damn, I was so strong fifteen minutes ago.* But there was something about this man. We jumped in his 745 and pulled off. It was 5:50 PM; I couldn't miss my flight. The first few minutes were silent because Emmet was in the car, and it was clear that we didn't like each other. It wasn't always that way—we used to all go to the movies together. Emmet would eat dinner and breakfast at our house; we would all sit on the couch and watch movies. He and Jerri would have me die laughing when they recited lines from "What's Love Got to Do with It." That was the good old days, but ever since Jerri and I had an altercation in front of him, he hasn't liked me. As you already know, I didn't give a fuck. There was always something about him that rubbed me wrong. One night, Jerri and I was talking as we usually did, and he told me that Emmet said that when they got rich-rich, he wanted to snort a line every now and then. That made him a weak ass nigga to me. His hating ass cost me a trip to be

Bahamas. I really didn't like him after that shit. He was a fucking hater and I didn't trust him, so I didn't speak around him at all. Jerri dropped him off on Alpine to some cookout.

"So where's the song?" It was Neyo, number eleven, "Let Go," then he played number five, "I Call Your Name." I was laughing. "You call my name? Boy, you're stupid."

"Shela, stay."

"I can't."

"Just stay for one night. I want to take you to my new spot."

"Jerri, I can't. I have to go home."

"Is he that important; is it that serious? Already?"

"What are you talking about, Jerri? There is no *he*!" I was lying through my teeth; I knew I could stay. Allen and I weren't serious, but I didn't want to fuck things up. "Look, I can't stay."

"How much is the bill? In fact, it doesn't matter. I'll give you six thousand dollars right now if you stay for one night."

"You not giving me shit. That hospital bill is $4,853. You're trying to make me miss my flight." I'd just noticed that we had been sitting at the same location for the past twenty minutes, right on the corner of Sherman Avenue and Bigelow Street. "The song was nice, but I have to go home, Jerri. I can't keep going in circles with you."

"Are you sure you can't stay for one night?"

"Yes, I'm sure. Please don't make me miss my flight, Jerri." It *was* nice, but I had to go home. He pushed the gas as if he couldn't wait to get me out of his car. We arrived at Newark International Airport in less then ten minutes. He pulled up to terminal C, door number 2; it was 6:50 PM. I hopped out of the car and hurried to the trunk to get my bags. With his attitude, I didn't expect him to help me, but he beat me to the trunk and pulled out my bags. "Thank you, Jerri. Bye."

"You're not going to give me a kiss, Shela?"

"Of course." I kissed his lips and instantly felt the water coming to my eyes. "I got to go. I love you." I couldn't let him see me cry. I walked swiftly into the airport, hoping he didn't notice my tears. The thought of staying crossed my mind as I entered the automated doors of Newark Liberty Airport. As I proceeded to the escalator, I heard Jerri shout my name. I turned around slow so that I could wipe my tears, thinking I had forgotten something. I looked directly at him, wondering what it could be; I was already moving upward on the escalator. He shouted, "I forgot to say I love you."

I didn't respond. I just darted off into the Security line. I didn't want to think about how bad I wanted to stay. I made it to the gate, just in time. The attendants announced that flight number 287 would be boarding in fifteen minutes. This gave me more time to contemplate my situation. I wished I could relive the past year. I wished I could erase his fuck-ups and fix it because I truly loved this man. He was good to me; he took great care of me. My love for him allowed me to make excuses for his fuck-ups. I decided to stay, but of course I had to call Allen to inform him, "Hey Allen, we're on the way to the airport but it seems like I'm going to miss my flight."

"What?"

"I think I'm going to miss my flight."

"Really? Try to make another flight."

"I'm booked on the last flight into Miami."

"Well, take a flight into Fort Lauderdale or Palm Beach. I'll pay the difference, and I'll be there to pick you up. Call and let me know what time you'll land."

Fuck! I really couldn't afford to fuck this one up, but I wanted to stay. I called Quan, "Quan, man!"

"Hello?"

"Quan."

"What happen? You okay?"

"Yeah, I'm good."

"You missed your flight?"

"No, not yet. I'm thinking about it."

"What? Girl, go home."

"I am. I'll call you when I land." Meanwhile, Jerri continued to call my phone. I didn't answer; I call Mimi instead, "Mimi, what do I do? Part of me—no, all of me—wants to stay."

"What are you talking about, Neshela?"

"Jerri wants me to stay. I want to stay, but what the hell will I tell Allen?"

"Neshela, you need to really think about what you're doing. Allen is a nice guy and he offer what you really want."

"Mimi, it's not the security; it's not like that yet."

"It not like that because you keep going back in forth with J. I'm going to tell you like I told him: the both of you underestimated each other and fell in love. Now ya'll don't know what to do. Do what you feel is right—follow you mind. Like you told me, your heart will always lead you wrong."

Just then the announcement came over the loudspeaker, "Now boarding all seats all rows, all seat, all rows are welcome to board at this time."

"Is that your flight?" Mimi must have heard.

"Yes. I really thought that I was over him."

"I guess not, girl."

"Well, that's him calling my other line. I'll call you later."

"Okay, bye." I hung up with Mimi and finally answered Jerri's call.

"Hello," I said, still not sure what to do.

"I know you didn't leave. I'll be at the airport in fifteen minutes to pick you up, okay?"

"Don't bother." I hung up and boarded my flight home. I couldn't stay.

Chapter 23

Still in Love

We talked regularly for the next two weeks, and he finally decided to pay half of the hospital bills. We planned to meet in Cancun for Memorial Day weekend.

Liz and I was going crazy trying to prepare for the trip. It was the last week of May. Our hotel called to inform us that we did not have a room for Thursday night because the travel agent double booked our room. I was able to work things out with Mack so he made sure we had a spot to lay our heads. We're counting down the days. Liz and I were so excited about the trip. She had planned several tours for us to enjoy while in Mexico. I was so ready to go. I was a little pissed because Allen had just added me to his American Express card and requested that one was rushed to me so that I could have it for my trip, but I had not received it yet.

That evening, I received a call from Jerri; he called to inform me that he would not be going to Mexico. He was pulled over a few days earlier and there was weight in the car. His man took the rap for everything, but it took the county jail a few days to release Jerri. He sounded stressed about the whole thing, so I didn't bother to ask any questions. I'm pissed. We planned this trip for a few weeks, and besides, I booked all his shit on my card. At this point, I didn't even want to go anymore, but I couldn't leave Liz hanging. Therefore, I went ahead and packed my bags.

Our flight was scheduled to depart at 11:30 AM from Fort Lauderdale International Airport. I decided to stay at Allen's house because he lived closer to the airport, and he was always my ride. On Thursday morning, it was a complete rush. We woke up 10:00 AM.

"Oh shit, Neshela. You're going to miss your flight."

"I can't miss my flight! Let's go."

We jumped in the Bentley GT Coupe and flew to the airport. It felt like he was going 130 miles an hour all the way there, and I made it just in time. Liz was already at the ticket counter when I arrived, so I walked right to the front and stood next to her. The ticket agent began to check me in, when she realized that my passport was of an eight–year-old little girl named Astar; I packed the wrong passport! And Liz was pissed because there no other flights to Mexico until Saturday, and there was no way that we were going to make this flight. It was a good thing that Allen usually waits for me to give him the okay before he leaves the airport. I was known for missing flights.

Allen appeared to be a little worried when I got in the car. He had a funny look on his face.

"What wrong with you?" I asked.

"Nothing, I just hope you don't ruin my weekend because you missed your flight. I like to hang out on *ghetto*-ass South Beach for Memorial Day." Miami has a big ghetto-day weekend, as I call it, but it is a real Memorial Day weekend event that they have on South Beach. It's just too hood for me; I hate it. Allen assumed that I was going to ruin his weekend—and, basically, I was because I'm a little selfish at times. Considering Liz was also pissed, I didn't have any plans on bothering her. So, as usual, I acted like a brat and went out with Allen and his niggas, but that didn't work out. I hated when Allen drank, and I refused to sit around and watch him drink bottle after bottle. So we went to a boutique on the beach to buy me a dress. I decided to hang out with my brother's girlfriend and her sister. The weekend didn't turn out that bad; I actually enjoyed myself with *Diamond Princess* and the girls.

Going back to Jersey was easy to pull off this time. I was staying for the weekend. We're all going to the Tarver and Mayweather fight in Atlantic City. Jerri and I had spoken a few times about attending the fight together, but neither of us followed up. In fact, we hadn't really talked much as the weeks passed. I decided to attend the fight with Quan and Mimi.

My flight landed in Newark at 1:00 PM. I called Quan to let him know that I was standing in front of door 3 at terminal C. Within minutes, Quan and his sister, Shelly, pulled up.

"Where is Mimi?" I asked. Quan informed me that at the last minute, Mimi changed her mind and decided to stay home with the baby. I nodded and turned to his sister. "Hey Shelly, how are you?"

It took her a second to respond, with a slight attitude, "I'm fine, how are you doing?"

"I'm good, girl."

Quan interrupted us. "Okay, y'all. We have two hours ahead of us. Do y'all need anything? I don't plan on stopping; everyone is already in AC." Neither of us wanted anything, but Quan brought us both water and juice from the gas station.

One hour and four minutes of just Neyo—this has to be the album of the year. We arrived in Atlantic City at 2:45 PM on the dot. After Quan checked everyone in the Hilton, the bellhop delivered our bags. Shortly afterward, we all headed to the table to gamble for a bit. I kept losing, and after five hundred dollars, I was ready to go. So Shelly and I walked the pier to people-watch; Atlantic City is full of people. But there was something different about Shelly; she had a slight attitude toward me, and I was dying to know why. When we returned to the room, Shelly laid everything out. "Neshela, after a day of kicking with you, you're a cool chick. But that shit you did at the baby shower wasn't cool."

"Girl, what are you talking about?"

"Why are you gonna be sitting next to Wesley? And Jennifer know that you fucking him."

"What the hell are you talking about, girl? I haven't talked to Wesley in over a year—he doesn't even have my phone number. At the baby shower was the first time that I seen Wesley in forever."

"Are you serious, Neshela? That lying-ass Wesley!"

"What happened? I want to know the story; what did he say?"

"Nothing, girl!"

"No, chick. I want to know. Let me hear this."

"Wesley made it seem like you was his girl and that he flew you up for the baby shower. He was at our table telling all of us how he got his chicks in check. Considering y'all was sitting next to each other, it made sense to us."

"Shut the fuck up." I was dying laughing, listening to Shelly telling this crazy-ass story. Wesley has a wild imagination. "Wesley, the fucking lair! His girl—what the fuck. Shelly, I stopped talking to Wesley a little after I started fucking with J. And I was never his girl."

"Oh, I ain't even know that you fuck with J! Now it all makes sense. I don't really know J, and I didn't know he was your dude. Wesley a lying ass. I should have known better."

"Yes, you should have. This is the second time I heard some bullshit with him. Wesley was telling some chick named Shawn some bullshit-ass story about me and him."

"Shawn who?"

"I don't know. J said that she was one of Monique's friends. The chick called J and told him the whole story. Girl, J and I was dying laughing. J had stopped talking to Monique and I wasn't talking to Wesley, so I guess these two fools was entertaining themselves, not knowing that the chick, Shawn, and J talk. Shawn know that J wasn't talking to Monique and that Monique didn't even have J's phone number, but she was fronting for Wesley, acting like Jerri was sweating her. So Wesley had to do the same thing, front for Monique and her friend, like I be calling him." I was laughing so hard. "He's a joke—a real clown. I'm good on that dude; I thought he was better than that."

"He going to the fight with us tonight?"

"I don't know, girl; I have no rap for Wesley. He just better not say shit to me."

"Girl, enough about Wesley's lying ass. Can I use your phone? I need to call my boyfriend down in Florida."

That evening, we all went to the fight, and of course I ran into Jerri; he's with his gang of niggas. I walked past him as if I didn't see him, making sure that he got a good look. The fight was crazy; it went twelve rounds. Mayweather whipped Tarver's ass. After the fight, we headed to 40/40, Jay-Z's club. Mack had reserved an upper room for the crew to party. We never made it in the club. It's crazy, and people were everywhere. So Rachel and I decide to do us. We went to the Crease and gambled, then we rolled through the Taj Mahal. I was hoping to see Jerri, but I didn't. We decided to end our night pretty early. We were getting tired of walking around in circles and losing money on the tables. We returned to Newark the following day, and of course, Jerri called. "Why didn't you call last night?"

"You know my number, Jerri; you could have called me!"

"I want to see you. You looked good last night."

"I know! What you expect? I always look good."

"You know, today would have been my son's birthday if you didn't—"

"If I didn't what? Kill him, is that what you want to say? Yes, I know it's June 12, and it would have been our son's birthday if I was sure about being with you."

"Yeah, whatever. Let me speak to Mimi."

"Hold on—Wait, no. Call her phone."

"Why? You don't want her to know that we talk?"

"Whatever, Jerri, hold on—Mimi, J wants you." They talked for a few minutes, then she handed me the phone back.

"I'm going to call you tonight. I want to sleep on phone with you. You better answer," he said.

"Whatever."

"I love you."

"Yeah okay, Jerri. Bye."

That night we slept on the phone like old times. That morning, I rode to the city with Mimi; we did a little shopping as usual. My flight was scheduled to depart at 4:30 PM, but on our way back Jerri called and asked me to stay for dinner. I accepted his dinner date and called Allen to inform him. "Hey, baby. I'm going to come home tomorrow. We decided to have a girl's night out. We're going to the city—it Rachel's birthday." I was lying my ass off, but I couldn't tell him the truth. He was fine with my plans. He instructed me to have fun and to be sure to get on the first flight back because he missed me.

Jerri met us at Shelly's house. After Jerri picked me up, we went to meet Mack. After leaving Mack's, Jerri took me to his new favorite spot, Cuban Pete's. He had told me all about it; it was a restaurant owned by a Miami native, Mr. Pete. It was obvious that they were expecting us. When we entered the restaurant the waiters and hostess greeted us; they were all familiar with Jerri. They greeted him as if he was one of the owners. I mumbled to him "I hope you haven't been here with anyone else."

"No, they know all about you, don't worry!" he assured me.

"Choose your table," the Cuban man shouts in a heavy accent. "You finally brought your wife. She's just as beautiful as you said; she's even prettier than the picture" He came over and looked at me. "Hello, you must be Mrs. Miami; I have heard so much about you. He's always here alone. I ask when he is going to bring his wife and finally, you're here. How is Miami?"

"It's great, thanks for asking."

"I'm from Havana, but I lived in Miami, Florida, for the past fifteen years. I just moved to New Jersey, about two years now. To open my restaurant. You'll enjoy your dinner at Pete's. Nice to meet you."

I ordered *pollo* and rice, and it was delicious. They served their drinks in a pitcher, mixed with fruit and sparkling cider. I truly enjoyed my dinner; the night was wonderful. I was sitting across the table from Jerri, having flashbacks of happier times when we were together. I was and missing him and all the little things we did. We'd talk all night and have dinner at our table; we used to sit on the couch playing Madden. I reminisced on how he used to read to me and on our long hours in the Jacuzzi. I was not over him and still loved him and missed being with him. After dinner, we checked in the Hyatt Regency on the Hudson River. We lay so close to each that night, as if we were one.

Instead of flying back to Miami, I flew to Atlanta where I was meeting Allen for dinner at the Sun Dial, located at the Westin downtown, which happens to be one of my favorite hotels. I planned to fly out of Atlanta that evening after dinner, but Allen had a surprise for me. He knew that the NJ Boyz would be in Miami for my birthday and that we planned to party for the entire weekend. I was turning twenty-five years old, and I had plans to have my first drink. Allen decided to take this time to celebrate my birthday a few days early. He booked a room at the Westin, on the fifty-fifth floor, with a breathtaking view of the city. Allen began telling me how special I was to him and presented me with a small box. I was extremely flabbergasted. I began pulling away the gold wrapper that covered the small box to reveal a 2-carat, VVS, princess-cut diamond ring inside. It's beautiful and elegant. I accepted it, but deep in the depths of my heart I knew that I shouldn't have. Along with the ring came promises that I couldn't fulfill, especially after the wonderful weekend Jerri and I shared. That night, Allen and I began talking about the past, the present, and the future, but unknown to him, I was still in love with my ex and there could be no future for us. We fell asleep, and I boarded my flight for Miami that morning. I was ready to party with Quan and the NJ Boyz. They were due in town late that evening. The entire weekend was planned out.

It was Sunday night at the Forge. We began celebrating Liz's birthday, and at midnight her birthday celebration ended and mine began. Our hostess brought us chocolate-swirl cake with vanilla ice cream, and the plates read "Happy Birthday." We drank bottle after bottle of Jose Cuervo Patron, and with each bottle of Patron, we were taking shots and singing "Happy Birthday." It was my goal to get drunk that night because it was my first and last time drinking alcohol. I didn't plan to drink again; like I've said, it's not my thing. Unfortunately, I found out that I don't get drunk. Rumor has it that I was drinking water instead of Patron.

The day after I celebrated my birthday with the NJ Boyz, it was time to break the news to Allen. I was back with Jerri and we were happier than ever. After my birthday, I flew back to Jersey to spend a week with Jerri. It was like old times again, except one of his little man was indicted for murder, and, on top of that, one of his stash houses kept getting hit up. Shit was different; he and Mike were no longer doing business together. Money wasn't the same, and he was stressing, mostly because of all the indictments that were going on in Newark. Shit was crazy in Jersey; niggas were getting picked up left and right. I was begging Jerri to do something different. I always wanted more. With the money we saved, we could make things happen. When Jerri used to give me an allowance, unknown to him, I saved most of it. I always wanted more for us, and since I decided to settle with a dope boy, I knew that I had to keep some coins in the bank. You never know what will happen, and I never planned to be that chick that didn't have enough to live anymore because my drug-dealer boyfriend went to jail or got killed. I kept enough money to maintain things, just in case anything happened.

Chapter 24

Getting Things Lined Up

It was the end of August when I suggested that we move to a more central location. The back-and-forth between Miami and Jersey was beginning to wear me out. Besides, I wanted to be next to him every night. It took us a few days to decide where we were going to build our home: Virginia, Atlanta, South Carolina, or Maryland. I did some research, and Atlanta and South Carolina offered the best prices and the most house for the money. We made a trip to both cities and Atlanta was our final choice. We spent the whole month of August going back and forth to Atlanta and finally we decided on a house in Alpharetta, Georgia. I fell in love with the community immediately. The houses were beautiful; they were all four-sided brick and stone. I whispered in Jerri's ear, "This is it!" We found a model of the house that I wanted.

After viewing the house, we went back to the Westin Hotel, where we were staying, and discussed our opinions. The house that we chose was over 5,500 square feet with six bedrooms, five bathrooms, three fireplaces, and the walk-in closet in the master bedroom was to die for. The total price was $659,000, but financially we were in a bind. Most builders in Georgia only required five to ten stacks to start the project, but John Willis homes required three installments of eighteen thousand dollars. It would take approximately nine months to build our home. The next morning, we met with the agent to execute the contract. I signed and dated the required documents; it was August 18, 2006. I finally felt that we accomplished something. Even though shit was still crazy in Jersey, we both had something to look forward to.

Another one of Jerri's boys was picked up, and one of his low spots was raided, but this time the cops found work. I begged Jerri to come to Miami and get away from all of the drama, but he wouldn't. He said he had a business to run, and he couldn't just leave. I was willing to go to Jersey, but he asked me not to come with everything going on. I didn't want to be in the middle of anything, but I was missing him. A few days seemed like months; by the end of the week, Jerri asked me to look into getting a place in Atlanta right away. He wanted to lie low for a few weeks. I contacted the agent for our house, and she suggested that we take advantage of the lease program that the builders offered, through a local apartment complex. At the rate we were paying for hotel accommodation, the discounted price for the apartment home was good. It was only 1300 square feet, but it served its purpose. It was our new getaway spot. I signed the lease on August the twenty-seventh. It was official. I planned to spend a few days in Atlanta getting things together, but it turned into a week of making sure everything was in place. I had a small budget of six thousand dollars to hook up the apartment, and I made it happen.

I flew back to Miami to take care of some business and to get Astar ready for third grade. While in Miami, I decided that I was ready to make Atlanta my new home. With all the wild shit going on in Jersey, I knew it would be a good move for Jerri. I just had to talk him into moving eight months earlier than the original plan. It would be hard, but I knew it was the best thing for us.

Jerri met me in Atlanta the following weekend. It was the first time that he seen our new getaway spot and the first time that we seen each other in weeks. I was so busy getting things together that I didn't realize that it had been that long. When I seen him at the airport, I'd realized that I missed the hell out of him. We immediately went home, and sex was the first thing on the agenda. It was the greatest sex ever.

Jerri flew back to Newark the following day, and I flew to Miami to get all of the documents needed to register Astar for school in Georgia. The first week in our new apartment was going well, and before I knew it, it had already been a month. Jerri was in and out of town, only spending a few days at a time in Atlanta, and I was starting to miss him. There was a sense of emptiness in our new apartment. Jerri had been attending a trial for the past week. I didn't know the details, and I didn't care. I just wanted him next to me. It was Thursday morning, October 12, when Jerri sent me a text that read, "I can't wait to see you I miss you better half." He was reading my mind.

Within seconds, my phone rang. "Hey baby," I answered.

"Shela," Jerri said softly.

"I need to see you. I miss you so much."

"I'll be home in few days. This trial shit is crazy, baby. I have to be here for my men, but I'll be home as soon as this is over, okay?"

"I hear you, but it's been two weeks already."

"Shela, I was just there. It hasn't been that long; I'll be home soon."

"My mother and grandmother are coming in town on

the twenty-ninth to spend some time with Astar for her birthday."

"Okay, well, they can stay at the house. Book us a room downtown at the Glen Hotel or the Westin."

"Okay. Do you want me to go ahead and book your flight too?"

"Yeah, baby, book it. Go ahead and book it for the twenty-seven I need to put my tongue in your ass."

"You're crazy."

"I just got to the courthouse. I'll call you in a few hours."

He surprised me and came home for the weekend. We didn't do much of anything—I was just so happy to see him. I hated not having him by my side every night. When we awoke on Saturday morning, we went to look at our house. It was still in the framing stage, but we were just happy to be looking at our accomplishment.

Just when I thought that things were going to be okay, I got a call on Saturday afternoon from Astar's godfather. I was on my way to the Lenox mall when he called to inform me that my nephew was just shot and killed. He didn't have any details, but he told me that he would keep me posted. I immediately called my mother. She had no clue, so I didn't bother to share the news. I called the ghost; he told me to stay by the phone, he'd call me right back. I called my mother again and finally told her what I had heard. Within a few minutes, we had the whole story.

My nephew was a victim of a home invasion. There was six victims; two were killed on the scene, four others were wounded, all in critical condition. My nephew was one of the four; his sister, mother, and aunt were the other victims. I fell to my knees. "*My God!* He's only five years old! Who could put a gun to the head of a five-year-old?" I lay on the couch crying; it was just a few years earlier when his father, my brother, was shot in the head. It was only the grace of God that spared his life. A few hours passed, and I called Jerri to inform him of what was going on with my family. I could tell he was at a loss for words. When he finally spoke, he said, "Baby, I'm gonna be on a flight in the morning. Where do you want me to meet you, Miami or Atlanta?"

"I'm not sure yet. I'm waiting to get more details; I'll keep you posted."

"I love you. Stop crying, man, it is going to be okay. Call me back so you can give me all the details. I love you; I'll be there."

"I love you too. Bye."

Within minutes, I received calls from everyone; even Allen called to check on me. I planned to travel to Miami that evening. My brother was locked up, so I planned to visit him right away. I knew he needed my support, but then my father called. He told me that the doctors at Jackson Memorial Hospital released a statement to the media and the family, stating that my nephew was not going to make it. Therefore, there was no sense in me flying down right away. I called Jerri and gave him all of the details. I also told him that I was okay and that I knew that he was still dealing with the trial, so he didn't need to rush home. His flight was already booked for the following week, and, besides, I knew he had to drive the BMW to South Carolina. Truly, at this point in my life, I thought I had been through it all.

The week went by slow, but it was finally time for me to see my man. It was the twenty-seventh of October. I had made an appointment for both of us to go to the spa. I was so ready for him to come home; it had been eight days since the last time I seen him. And his stay only lasted for a day the last time he was in town.

I called Jerri and got his voice mail. "Hey baby. I was just calling to give you the details on your flight. You're on flight number 173. It leaves Newark at 3:30 PM. I can't wait to see you; I miss you. Call me when you get this." My man was coming home and I planned to have my Freakum Dress on. While standing in the mirror, imagining that Jerri was behind me, my cell phone rang. It was the Bow Wow and Ciara ring tone—Jerri. "Hey baby, you at the airport?" I asked.

"I missed my flight."

"*What?*"

"Some shit come up that I got to take care of. Just re-schedule it for Tuesday, baby. I got to take care of this. I'll make it up to you, I promise. I'll be here for a while. I got to get down there and chill for a minute, baby. Shit is still crazy up here."

"What's going on, Jerri?"

"It's nothing. Don't worry; I'll talk to you when I get down there."

"Okay."

"Uh, Shela, when is the money due on the house, and how much is it?"

"It not due until January; it's only eighteen thousand dollars."

"Okay, how much is in the safe?"

"Yours or mine?"

"Both."

"I don't know, I'll check. Maybe thirty, no more than that."

"You don't have to check. I was just making sure the house money was good. I'm gonna put some cash in your PNC account okay?" He was quiet for a second, and then he changed the subject. "What's going on with your nephew; they didn't pull the plug, right?"

"No, he moved his hand earlier this week. He's still in a coma, but he'll make out—he's strong like his dad," I said.

"Shit, that's crazy."

"I know; I feel so sorry for his mother. Both of her children are in critical condition. My God, I don't think I could handle that, Jerri."

"We won't have to. I'll see you on Tuesday. Love you."

"Love you too. Talk to you later, baby." It was an early night for me; I lost all my energy since Jerri wouldn't be home. It was another weekend of long, lonely nights.

I wanted to be first to say "Happy birthday," so I left our song on his voice mail—Bow Wow and Ciara's "Like You." That was our code to call each other, and indeed he called back right away.

"What's wrong?" he asked.

"Happy Birthday to you, happy birthday to you, happy birthday, my baby—"

He laughed. "Shela, shut up! You sound horrible, but I love you."

"I love you too. I'm on my way to a closing; I'll call you in a few hours. I just wanted to say 'happy birthday.' I have a busy day ahead of me; I'm closing my first deal in Atlanta."

"That what's up, Ms. Mortgage Broker! Get that money, baby! I'll call you when I get in the house tonight. It'll be late; don't wait up for me."

"Where you going? Out, tonight?"

"We went out last night; we're probably going to the city tonight," he said.

"Okay, now."

"Baby, I'll call you tonight."

"Be safe."

I woke up at 1:00 AM, but I didn't have any missed calls from Jerri, so I went back to sleep. I woke again at 3:00 AM.

My stomach was killing me like when I was pregnant with Moon. I got out of the bed in tears, the pain was so intense. I called Jerri, but no answer. I figured that he was in the club and couldn't hear his phone ring. So I didn't bother to call again. I just curled up in the bed and rocked myself to sleep.

Chapter 25

Talking to God

I woke up thinking it was a beautiful day. Those thoughts came to a fast end. I was so busy getting things ready for Astar's birthday, I didn't realize that my cell phone was off. I hated this Pocket PC; the touch screen was so sensitive. I had seventeen missed calls: ten from Mimi, five from Quan, and two from a New Jersey number that I didn't know. It was about noon when I received the Call. It was Mimi. "Neshela, where are you?"

"I'm shopping for stuff. It's Astar's birthday. What's up, chick? I just tried to call you. I seen I missed a few calls from you."

"I need to talk to you, girl."

"Mimi, did you talk to J today?"

"Neshela, sit down. I need to tell you something."

"What's wrong Mimi? Where is Quan? What happened?" I knew something had to be wrong but I never thought for a second ...

"It's not us. It's you! Sit down."

"Tell me what's wrong! What happened, Mimi? *What happened?*"

"They found J dead in his car around 10:00 AM, we been trying to call you all morning."

"Stop lying; you got to be lying!"

"I'm sorry; I'm sorry."

"Mimi, please tell me you're lying. I just talked to him—I just talked to him yesterday, I wished him a happy birthday. I called him twice last night, he didn't answer …" I felt like I wanted to faint.

I knew I would never be the same after this tragedy, but I had to be strong. *Today is Astar's birthday.* The tears won't stop, they keep coming—*my God, what could have happened?* I called Quan immediately, "Quan, what happened?"

"Nobody knows yet," he said.

"Quan, please tell me what happened."

"Give me a minute."

"Quan, I got a know what is going on."

"I'm going to call you right back."

"No, tell me now please!"

"Answer the phone—I'm going to call you right back."

"Okay." It was a matter of seconds before the phone rang. Of course I picked up immediately. "What happened, Quan, what happened?"

"Shit, we don't know yet. I'll let you know when I know something."

I immediately called Liz; I needed to talk to someone. "Liz, Jer … Jerr … erri was killed today," I stammered.

"Oh my god! Are you okay? Do you need me to come there? I can be on a flight right away."

"No, give me a chance to see what I'm going to do. What will I do without him, Liz? What will I do?"

"We'll make it. Everything will be okay, girl. It will be okay. Where is Astar?"

"At school. My mom is calling, I'll call you right back."

"Okay, call me, girl."

I hung up with Liz and picked up my mom's call. She started talking before I could say hello. "Neshela, I been trying to call you all day. Have you talked to Mimi? Neshela, it's going to be okay, baby. Mimi told me what happened. Are you okay?"

"NO! I'm not okay!"

"You need to get on a flight and come home, baby."

"I'm home, mom. I'll be okay."

"This is your brother on the other line. I'll call you right back." Within seconds the phone rang; it was my mother calling back. "Ay, baby. It's going to be okay. You got to be strong, sis. Okay?" The tears flowed hard when I heard my brother's voice, 'cause indeed this could have been him. He said, "Baby, that how this game goes. I know you don't want to hear this, but it's the truth. Pull yourself together and be strong. Sometimes I wish I was dead!"

"Rob, don't say that!" Mom yelled.

"Mom, this jail shit ain't no joke. Shela, you have to keep living. Keep living, Shela."

I went in the house and surrounded myself with pictures. All I had were my memories to hold onto. I received a few more calls before Astar arrived home from school. I put on my happy face and like any good mother, I played the role. "Happy birthday, baby!" It was my baby's ninth birthday. I decided that it would be best if we got out of the house. I took her to the Cheesecake Factory for dinner. As we sat at the table, the phone rang again.

"Hey, Neshela."

"Yes, who this is?" I asked.

"Melissa."

"Oh, hi."

"Malik called me—he was trying to get in contact with you. It took me a minute to locate someone in Miami with your number. Sorry about your nephew, but that's not what I called about. I called to tell you that J was killed today."

"I already know."

"Is it okay for me to give Malik your number?"

"Sure."

"I know you're alone here, but remember, I live in Atlanta too, so if you need anything feel free to call me."

"I will, thank you." I hung up, but I couldn't stop the tears.

"Mommy what's wrong, what happened?" Astar asked.

"Nothing, baby."

"Why are you crying, Mommy?"

I took a deep breath. "Baby, I need to tell you something. Today, Mr. J got killed."

Astar came to my side. "Mommy, it's going to be okay. I'll help you."

When we returned home, Astar opened her birthday gift and we celebrated the best that we could under the circumstances. I tucked her in bed and went straight to my room. I had to talk to God.

"God, please, why me? Why? I have never questioned you before, but I don't understand this one. God, I need to see him, I want to talk to him; you got to let me talk to him, God. I miss him, God. I miss him already. I can't live without him; I would give up heaven for one day with him. God, I need him more than you know. I never thought I would be without him—you didn't even warn me. You took him—why? I can't even talk to him. I don't have a choice, and that's not fair!"

The next few days revealed all types of things. The stories were crazy. Jerri's death was caused by an oral gunshot wound, which appeared to be suicide. I couldn't believe it—Jerri killed himself.

"I miss him, God. It's been four days, the darkest four days of my life. I haven't slept, ate, or bathed in the last four days. All I can think of is him and our memories."

All of the what-ifs crossed my mind and played over and

over. What if I had our kids? What if he was here? What if I called him at 1:00 AM instead of 3:00AM? What if I just kept calling? What if I talked to him, could I have changed his mind? What if I was there instead of here?

No, I didn't feel guilty. I felt empty; I have never been in love the way I was with him. I love him because he always put me first, no matter what. He made sure that I was happy. It's so hard for me to let go. I decided to write to Jerri every night. It was my way of talking to him, my therapy.

Indeed, shit got crazy and the stories were changing by the minute. First, he found out he had AIDS and killed himself. Of course that was some bullshit. Then I heard he was depressed and going broke so he killed himself. The last story I heard was that there was a hit placed on the lives of his family members for money that he owed. Therefore, he took his life to save theirs. The best story came from an anonymous call. When I answered my cell phone, it was a male voice. He said, "If I was you, I would not be in Jersey this weekend. Shitara told the detective that you are Jerri's connection, and because of money owed to your family there was a threat placed on the lives of his family members and you were fully aware. Your flight leaves at 9:20 AM on Friday morning—Continental flight number 103. The detectives will be there to take you for questioning—you better bring your lawyer."

"Who is this?"

"The only reason I called was to warn you. I know Jerri wouldn't want that for you."

"Who is *this*?" The voice faded away, and the minutes on my phone stopped. *Wow, what could have made her do this? How can she put me in some bullshit like this?* I didn't know what to do. I'm not sure if I should call my lawyer to figure out the whole thing, or if I should just let time deal with it.

Now I was concerned—this bitch just put me in the middle of this mess. I packed my bags anyway; I had to say good-bye, I needed closure.

A part of me didn't believe that Shitara told the story. I thought that when Shitara and I spoke earlier that year, we had an understanding that I wasn't going anywhere. It seemed that someone was trying to change the focus of this whole tragedy and redirect the attention toward me but I couldn't understand why or who. I decided to let time deal with the matter.

Jerri's mother decided to make the funeral private—for whatever reason, she didn't feel safe, and I can't blame her. She only allowed close friends and family members; therefore our mutual friends from the crew didn't attend Jerri's homecoming service. They decided to take their pre-viously planned trip to Vegas, and I decided to stay home. It was the safest place for me, considering I again heard the same story that the anonymous caller had told me two days earlier.

Chapter 26

Letters to Jerri

I picked up a new habit. I couldn't let go, so I began to write Jerri every day as if he was here, as if I was really talking to him. I took my book everywhere so that I didn't miss a chat with my soul mate—the one man that gave me everything, the one man that put nothing in front of me. I couldn't let go of him.

November 1, 2006
I guess everything happen for a reason Jerri. That the easiest way for me to deal with this whole thing. I don't believe you did it to yourself, but I can't believe someone did this to you. I'm torn baby I really don't know what to believe. If you did it you did. I just wish you're here, I wish you would have called me. I hear you call some people, why didn't you call me? When I talked to you that morning why didn't you say anything? Why didn't you give me a hint?
November 3, 2006
The twins would have been two months today. What would I have done alone with three kids? Jerri ...

November 4, 2006
So today is your day. You're going to Heaven right? You better be there when I get there nigga.

November 10, 2006

I talk to Abdul today he sounded so distant at first, he made me feel uncomfortable. He doesn't believe that you did it to yourself, I really don't know Jerri. I don't understand anything about this whole situation. Abdul said that it is hard for him right now. He said that he tired of talking about it. He also said that the only reason that he answered the phone was because of you! He said "Neshela, I really don't want to talk about it anymore. I knows how much J cares about you that the only reason that I'm talking to you now." I asked him about the bullshit story. You know, that shit they say Shitara did. He said that he didn't hear anything like that.

November 12, 2006

I try to read a book the other day, I couldn't even get pass the first page. I couldn't stop crying. All I could think of is how you use to read to me. You spoiled the shit out of me. I can't even read for myself. I really miss you and all the things that we did.

Better half

November 13, 2006

Remember when you're crazy ass use to throw away your boxers and t-shirts. Talking about you make too much money to wear the same underwear twice. You just didn't have a washing machine …. Whatever Mr. I miss you, yo!

November 16, 2006

I want to come see you. I'm going to call Abdul and get the information. Maybe I'll come this weekend. I'll keep you posted.

November 19, 2006

I talk to Abdul, I asked him for the cemetery information so that I can come and see you. He said that you don't have a tombstone, and that it would be hard for me to find you. He said that he going to see you this weekend and that I can go with him. I'm going to try I can't make any promise. It Wednesday and I don't think I have enough time to make arrangement. I don't understand why you don't have a tombstone. I asked him how much does it cost, he said between $1000–$1800, he also said that your mom run out of money and because your death is a suicide the insurance didn't pay out. Jerri I told him that I would pay for the tombstone. He said he'll let your mother know.

He really doesn't believe that you commit suicide. That nigga really love you. I just don't know. J, I miss you, I wish you were here but I just don't know. I don't want to sell you short baby. I don't want to believe that you did this to yourself, if you didn't but I can't except that someone did this to you and no one try to figure it out. Suicide hurts but murder is a different story and murder that made to look like suicide is scary. I'm going to sleep, I love you.

November 23, 2006

Just thinking about you! I wonder how Jason doing? I don't know why but he crossed my mind today. I know it's hard for him Jerri, I was eleven when my father died it was hard. Happy Thanksgiving baby, I'll never forget last year your crazy ass mom. That shit was funny as hell. Her cabbage gave me high blood pressure. Okay let me stop. Neiman Marcus is having a big sale tomorrow. I wish you could go with me, I know you miss the fitting room …. The fun we used to have in the fitting room at Shore Hills.

December 2, 2006

Where you at fool? I'm sitting here looking at a pic of you. You know the one when you were talking on the phone with me; Sitting on the block looking sexy as hell.

December 13, 2006

I went shopping today for the first time in forever. I was at your favorite so I got a lot off bullshit it getting cold up here and I bought some shoe from Gucci .... No I didn't spend that much money only $3,500. I wish you could have help me pick clothes today.

December 17, 2006

Just thinking about you, love always!

December 20, 2006

LOST ... I MISS YOU.

What's up Mr. it's been a minute since we talked. I miss you Jerri what happen? Did you do this to yourself or did someone do this to you? Talk to me I' m open and I'm listening. I want to know, you have to give me a sign a clue tell me something baby. I need you to talk to me. I love you

December 25, 2006

Wow it's already Christmas. Remember last year at Disney. We had a ball—you and Jason was killing those turkey legs. I just watch the video of us in Disney. I miss you

December 27, 2006

I miss you but I have to do away with this therapy I'm beginning to feel crazy. GOODBYE I love you better half.

Where do I go from here? I wondered. *I have spent the last two months writing to a dead man.*

My God, help me! I have no plan — in fact, for the first time in my life I have no goals. It's almost New Year's and I don't even have any New Year's resolutions. I just wake up every morning, get Astar off to school, and go to sleep; that's all. I might as well be dying.

When the Realtor called to inform me that it was time for the next payment, I just wrote the check. I didn't even think about it. I didn't realize it was already January 13, 2007.

February 13, 2007

I know it been a long time since we talked.

I can't stop the tears they just keep coming all by themselves. I love you and miss you so much. I realize how depress I am, just four month ago I had everything; I mean everything and now it's all gone. I am good financially, but mentally, physically, and emotionally I'm fucked up. I'm not hurting for any money; I have enough cash in the safe to survive for a minute. The $18,000 for the house put a dent in my pockets but I'm still surviving. My room is like a vampire den is. I spend most of the day sleeping. Damn I wish you were here! I'm in a city where I don't know anyone and I don't know what you want me to do about the house. I couldn't dare to live in it and I won't share our dreams with anyone nor can I afford it alone. The mortgage will be $5,700. I know you saying I can do it! But I can't really I can't. I haven't closed any deals in a minute and plus the market is at a true stand still.

It is time for me to get my life back. I'm leaving tomorrow I'm going to Miami.

Chapter 27

Closing the Doors

Life must go on. The Super Bowl was in Miami. This was a great opportunity for me to get out. "My flight lands at 6:45 PM at Ft. Lauderdale International Airport, Mommy. Don't be late."

"I won't! So you staying with us, right?"

"No, I'm staying with Christopher."

"You two might as well get married, how long has it been? Seven years?"

"Mommy, please, we're just friends."

"Neshela, Jerri isn't coming back, baby. You have to move on."

"It's only been a few months! Damn, Mom!"

"Well, I'll be on time. Don't worry."

Of course she was late—twenty minutes late, at that.

"Sorry I'm late, baby. It is so much traffic." I didn't bother to respond, I'm just happy to be in Miami—the palm trees and the clear skies. I'm home again.

"Who my number one grandbaby?" my mother asked. Astar responded, " Me, Grandma, me!" She missed Miami just as much as I did. It was really nice to be home. I spent the day riding around sightseeing, as if I was a tourist. So many things had changed since the last time I was in Miami, but within an hour, it was like old times. I met up with Kenny and Christopher at Christopher's waterfront condominium on Sunny Isle, where I planned to stay for the next few days, and of course hatin'-ass Kenny had something to say. "So Shela, you just come in town and get keys to the house and the Range Rover; you're a bad bitch! You still weak for her, Chris."

"Kenny, you're crazy!" Chris said with a smile on his face.

"Well, look. I have the whole weekend planned for us. Both of my breezy are in town, so I'm going to need you to babysit for me. But I'm going to sponsor everything," Kenny said.

"Sorry, I don't have time to babysit, your corny-ass bitch. I plan to party this weekend." I had to make myself clear. I really wanted to have fun this weekend.

"We're going to party, Neshela. I booked three rooms on the beach for us. We're going to party, and I'm working on Super Bowl tickets right now."

"Look, Kenny. I already have a Super Bowl ticket; my uncle has a box. You're going need some better shit than a room on the beach, nigga," I shouted. I really had no plans on going the Super Bowl. Football wasn't the same without Jerri and the kids.

"Damn! Okay, we can go shopping tomorrow."

"Bal Harbor!" I shouted.

"Come on, Shela, I ain't fucking you," Kenny said. "Bal Harbor! Girl, you crazy … okay! Okay, Bal Harbor."

"Okay, *cake daddy!*"

Oh, by the way, Kenny and Christopher had grown up. They were not your college boys anymore; Kenny is now a computer engineer and makes about $190,000 a year, and Christopher owns a car dealership and several houses and a duplex in the city of Miami.

It was our late night of party, Sunday night at the Forbes. I was driving the 645, and Kenny and Christopher was driving the Range. We pulled up to the Forbes; it was crazy, people everywhere—it is definitely the place to be. After valet parking the cars, we walked straight to the front of the line. Michelle, Kenny's chick, knows the owner and I know the promoter, so we had no plans to stand in line. In fact, I don't do line; I had already secured our names on Mitch's list earlier that day. I walked right up and said, "Neshela Jones, party of four. I'm on Mitch's list."

"Can I see your ID?"

"Sure!"

"Okay Ms. Jones, give me one second. Let me get a hostess for y'all." Within a few seconds, a hostess escorted us into the club. I had a ball all weekend, and both of Kenny chicks turned out to be cool girls.

It was my last day in Miami and the most important day. I'm going to see my nephew for the first time since the home invasion. He recovered well; you would never know that he was shot in the head at point-blank range. He is normal, like any other child, running, playing, and full of energy.

It was time to return to Atlanta, my new home. I had a good time in Miami, but I missed Atlanta; I missed my peaceful home. The trip to Miami was good for my soul; I returned to Atlanta with a new outlook on life. I finally took my brother's advice and began to live again. It's a new day; I got up and took Astar to school, and then I decided to go to the gym. After the gym, I went to the bookstore. I had to change my focus and get my mind right. Therefore, I needed reading materials to get on track; I needed my swagger back. I hadn't made any real money in the past five months. I decided to spend the next few weeks working on me and getting myself back together: mind, body, and soul.

On my way home from the bookstore, I noticed the mail

truck, which reminded me that I hadn't checked the mail-box in weeks. Liz had reminded me to take care of the bills so I didn't have to worry, so when Jerri died, I paid all the bills up for nine months. Liz and I both had a lesson on blowing large amounts of money in short periods of times. I couldn't afford for that to happen. So I made sure that the bill were paid. Therefore, I didn't check the mailbox that often. It was usually just junk mail, anyway. I opened the box to find a notice from the post office informing me that I haven't check my mailbox in over fourteen days—as if I didn't know! The consequence for not checking the mailbox was a road trip to the post office. I had to pick up my mail directly from there. There was no sense in putting it off, so I turned around and made the drive. I had mail posted since January; it seemed like there was no end to the sealed envelopes. I completely forgot that back in December I'd put in the change of address for my Miami and Jersey addresses. I had so much mail to read.

As I got closer to the end, I noticed an envelope from New York Life, my insurance company. The letter was to inform me that the annual payment for our life insur-ance policy was due. I had totally forgotten! When Jerri and I agreed to the IVF, back in December of 2005, we also agreed to have insurance policies for each other, worth a total of one million dollars, in case anything happened to either of us. I wanted to be sure that our kids would be taken care of. The letter was dated January 18, 2007; it was originally mailed to our Jersey address. The next letter was from PNC bank, informing me that there was no activity on our existing accounts and that the bank had been trying to contact us. First I called the insurance company to can-cel Jerri's accidental-death insurance and to see if I could get a refund for five months of payment, given that Jerri had died in October. The insurance agent assured me that

I could get a refund for the five months. However, he said I would need to fax a copy of the death certificate and incident report from the police station in order for him to adjust my account. It seemed a little unreasonable for a few hundred dollars. Next I contacted the bank, since I had no plans on going back to Jersey. I requested that they close the account and mail the balance of $9,832.03 directly to me. However, since both Jerri's name and my name was on the account, they needed notary consent from both parties to be completed before they could release the funds. I informed the young lady that Jerri was deceased, and there no way that he could complete the form. The bank rep promptly informed me that in order for the bank to release the funds, I would have to provide a certified copy of Jerri's death certificate. Where the hell was I supposed to get this? Great! I wasn't ready to go back to Jersey, so I just put it on the back burner.

It was already April, and the house was almost ready. At this point, I had no clue as to what I was going to do. It seemed like the year was flying by. I still hadn't closed any deals, so technically I hadn't made any money, and my Miami shopping spree was not helping my case. The safe money was getting lower and lower; thank God my bills were paid up until August. With my money getting low, I couldn't help but to think of the nine g's in the PNC account. After three weeks of reasoning with myself, I finally decided to go back to Newark to close some chapter of my life. But before I could move on, I opened a few new doors.

To be continued in …

Sunshine through Darkness

Sunshine

through

Darkness

Chapter 1

Opening New Doors

It was Friday, April 20, and I landed at Newark Liberty International Airport around noon. It was my first trip back to dirty Jersey. Ivan picked me up; we spent three hours riding around the city. I wanted to reminisce, so I asked Ivan to drive me to every location that he had ever taken Jerri and me. He granted my wish, and pulled out his little black book. Ivan's book contained every location that he'd ever driven us to, including the dates and times. He kept a detailed log for billing purposes, and I was grateful for that!

Jerri who made all the rules is no longer alive; therefore the rules that were previously laid out for me by him do not apply. I didn't have to use Angela to drive me in the hood, for that reason I had Ivan drive me to Mimi's salon. I didn't tell anyone that I was coming to Jersey, so Mimi was surprised to see me.

"Aw, Neshela! What are you doing here? Why didn't you call me?"

"I wanted it to be a surprise," I told her. We gave each other big hugs.

"It been so long; you okay?" she asked.

"I'll be okay. It's been hard, but it's time."

"I know," she said. "So when are you going to visit him?"

"Today. I got to talk to him; I miss him, Mimi."

"I know, me too. Your driver brought you here?"

"Oh, shit. I forgot about Ivan"

"Here are the keys; the truck is out front. I know you better be staying with us. You need help with your bags?"

"No, Ivan will do it. Yes, I'm staying with you, Mimi."

Mimi's best friend, Rachel, and her cousin Nancy arrived at the salon shortly after; it was like old times. We declared that Saturday will be girls' night out. Even though my trip was for Jerri, I welcomed the invitation. I hadn't partied since my twenty-fifth birthday celebration in Miami, at the Forbes. I needed to unwind. It felt good being back in Jersey.

I spent Friday evening at Rachel's house. We lay on the floor reminiscing on the good old days. I don't know how we got on the topic of suicide, but it brought tears to my eyes. At that moment, Rachel pulled an aqua book off her shelf, titled *Conversations with God: Book 1, Volume 2*. "Neshela, you should look at this one. I lost completely lost it after my mother died, and this book really touched my soul. It might help you." She handed me the book and exited the room. Without delay, I opened the book and went directly to the index: *suicide, death, communicating with the dead, darkness,* and *love.* I read each section, and it felt like I was finally feeding my soul; I hadn't done this in years.

The weekend flew by; before I knew it, it was Monday morning. I planned to spend most of the day with Jerri because I didn't make it to the grave site on Friday. For that reason, I was at the cemetery the minute they opened. I was hoping I was at the wrong place; that's how bad it was. They could have buried him anywhere else; shit, they could have buried him in the backyard. The cemetery was located on Central Avenue and Thirteenth Street. Shit couldn't get any worse than this; I wouldn't bury my dog at that cemetery. To make matters worse, Jerri didn't even have a tombstone. A bottle of Patron marked his spot! *Wow.*

After laying two dozen red roses and a mixed spring flower arrangement on his grave, I returned to the office of the cemetery. "I would like to purchase a tombstone for Jerri Hopkins, grave number two, row number fifty-three," I said.

"Well, the prices range from $800 to $1750," the man in the office said.

"I don't care how much it costs; he doesn't have a tombstone. The price doesn't matter."

"I'm sorry, miss, just a moment; I have to pull the file. What's your name?"

"Neshela! Neshela Jones."

"I'm sorry, Miss Jones, but I can't sell you a tombstone. Only Mrs. Ilene Hopkins can order it."

"That's fine. Can I just leave the money? You can call his mother and tell her to pick whatever she wants; I just want him to have a tombstone."

"Miss, I can't take your money; it's our policy. You will have to contact her, and she will have to be here to place the order."

I began to get flustered. "I just want him to have a tombstone, sir."

"I understand, miss, but it's our policy; I'm sorry. You can try calling the funeral service company; they may be able to help you."

"Thanks!" I said, and I left the cemetery. I called Woody Funeral Home, and they relayed the same information. I decided to call Abdul, but he didn't answer. *What a shame,* I thought. *Even if his family can't afford to pay for a tombstone, where the fuck is all these niggas from the block running around, talking about Alpine and the Firm and that Jerri is the mayor?*

They couldn't come up with $800 for a tombstone but they could have R.I.P party? How soon do people forget all about you!

Of course Abdul called back, and I asked, "Why doesn't Jerri have a tombstone?"

"Neshela, his mom didn't buy one. I guess she couldn't afford it."

"I told you months ago that I will pay for the tombstone. Can you call his mother and tell her that I will pay for the tombstone? I left my number with the cemetery; all she has to do is call and chose what she wants. I'll pay for it!"

"I'll call her, and I'll call you back." He never called back.

It was time to go home, but before I left, I had to make a trip to City Hall to get the documents that I came to Newark for in the first place. When I arrived at City Hall, I was second in line. I received the document that I requested within a matter of minutes. The young lady at the window handed me a sealed envelope that read: "Newark Division of Community Health". She instructed me where to get the other document that I'd requested. I didn't bother to unseal the envelope; I already knew the cause of Jerri's death was suicide. I followed the young lady's instructions, which led to the records department. After ten minutes of going back and forth with the officer who stood behind the bulletproof glass, I became upset. Newark's system is ancient.

"Miss, are you sure you have the right date?" he asked.

"Yes, sir. October 30."

"You said it was a suicide, right?"

"Yes, sir. Suicide. And his name is J-E-R-R-I Hopkins."

"Miss," the officer said, "I can't find anything with the information that you're giving me. You have to go upstairs to headquarters."

"Upstairs where?"

"Take the elevator up to the fifth floor, make a left, and

go down the hallway. The glass double doors will be on your left. Someone there will assist you; I'll call upstairs and give them the information that you gave me. Good luck!"

I moved quickly to the elevator; I had a flight to catch. I followed his directions to headquarters. When I entered the double doors, a female clerk rudely greeted me. I was not sure to what her issue was, but I tried my best to ignore her ill manners; she knows not what she do. "I just need a copy of a police report," I told her.

"What is the case number?"

"I don't have the case number, ma'am."

"What do you need a copy of the police report for?"

"Excuse me?"

"You're requesting a copy of a homicide report; *what do you need it for?*"

"I'm requesting a copy of a *suicide* report!"

"You are the young lady that records send here, right? You want a copy of Jerri Hopkins's report, *right?*"

"Yes!"

"Have a seat. A detective will be right with you."

My heart was racing at this point—a detective, a homicide. *What the hell is she talking about?* I unsealed the envelope and quickly scanned the page. "Box 29. Death due to: Pending investigation."

Oh my god. I am sitting in the lobby of homicide headquarters, and here comes this bitch again.

"*What's* your name again?" she asked.

"Look, lady, I don't have time for this. I have a flight to catch."

"Oh, you have time."

I needed to get the hell out of there; I was just about to curse this bitch out when a male voice interrupted us. "Are you Neshela Jones?"

"Yes, why?"

"Miss. Jones, "You have the right to remain silent. If you give up that right, anything you say can and will be used against you in a court of law. You have the right to an attorney and to have an attorney present during questioning. If you cannot afford an attorney, one will be provided to you at no cost. During any questioning, you may decide at any time to exercise these rights, to not answer any questions or make any statements. Do you understand the rights I have just read to you? With these rights in mind, do you wish to speak to me?"

Coming Soon...

The Death of a Legend

Sunshine through Darkness

Corner Boy